T. K. Hervey

Snooded Jessaline

The honour of a House - Vol. 3

T. K. Hervey

Snooded Jessaline
The honour of a House - Vol. 3

ISBN/EAN: 9783337195441

Printed in Europe, USA, Canada, Australia, Japan

Cover: Foto ©Andreas Hilbeck / pixelio.de

More available books at **www.hansebooks.com**

SNOODED JESSALINE

OR

THE HONOUR OF A HOUSE.

BY

MRS. T. K. HERVEY.

IN THREE VOLUMES.

VOL. III.

LONDON:

SAUNDERS, OTLEY, AND CO.

66 BROOK STREET, W.

1865.

CONTENTS

OF

THE THIRD VOLUME.

———◆◇◆———

SNOODED JESSALINE.

CHAPTER I.

BREAKING DOWN.

I knew that it must be!
Yea! thou art changed—all worshipped as thou art,
Mourned as thou shalt be! Sickness of the heart
Hath done its work on thee.
WILLIAM MACKWORTH PRAED.

Oh, to love less what one has injured! Dove,
Whose pinion I have rashly hurt,   *   *   *
Shall my heart's warmth not nurse thee into strength?
Flower I have crushed, shall I not care for thee?
Bloom o'er my crest my fight-mark and device!
ROBERT BROWNING.

ALL the household were looking forward to the coming of Lady Letty and her young charge. Lady Letty was looked upon at Fairfield as a sort of fairy godmother, ready and able at all times to perform faithfully the functions of that individual myth, and at the shortest notice. In the present case

Marian Favrel stood in the relation of the new-made princess that was to be; the only thing wanting now was the glass slipper, the ball, Heine Favrel for prince, the wedding ring, and the wedding. And fair, earnest, stately Marian was really no bad representative of the model princess.

The time which rolled over between the coming of the twins to our house, and the day which was to welcome the beloved travellers, had been marked by no occurrence of any moment. Heine continued somewhat moody; but the Colonel and I kept him well in hand between us, and he had improved a little; but there seemed to be something weighing on Heine's mind in connection with Marian. We encouraged his confidence, without seeming to force it, but beyond now and then a vague hint that there was something we should be told by-and-by we were yet in the dark. As for Walter, except for some trouble about Heine, he would have been perfectly happy. He was never weary of obeying the beck and call of his little tormentor, Ella, who seemed to have installed him in his Fairfield kennel as her tall, lithe Newfoundland pet, who was expected to fetch and carry for her, attend her in all her gambols, and bear the brunt of all the mischief she might get into. He certainly was a most devoted servitor, frank, fearless, and with just that sort of open-hearted forgetfulness of self which led us to suspect that Ella's liking for him arose from her seeing something in his manner which reminded her of Captain Flemming.

Towards each other the brothers were most devoted. This is generally the case with twins; and a very beautiful thing Ralph and I thought it. The differences in their minds and tempers seemed to draw the tie of affection closer instead of widening it. Each seemed to find in the other what he was conscious of missing in himself. Walter's buoyancy of temperament refreshed Heine, while Heine's steadiness gave a little balance to Walter. The same books pleased them both — oddly enough it seemed at first sight. But the explanation was a simple one. They were both, it will have been seen, a little one-sided in character, from the very accident of their birth perhaps; and one-sided people only see one side, only take one view of a subject: so that each selected for especial attention what pleased him best in any work he read, passing lightly over the rest; and what one brother discarded the other took to heart. It was like offering a sieve full of various seeds to birds of different habits: each pecked out what his nature needed, leaving his fellow-feeder's portion not one jot diminished.

This explanation of the perfectly harmonious accord between the brothers, and their entire devotion to one another, may serve also as an explanation of that perfect sympathy, or likeness in difference, which lay at the root of our own happiness, Ralph's and mine. His romantic sensibility balanced my matter-of-fact tendencies; his sweet melting tenderness of manner, my somewhat self-contained coldness; his generosity, my cautiousness; his spirit of self-sacrifice, my —— well, I am only giving my own view of the matter: he says I have no power of reading character. He told me so when I made this remark to him; and as I always think women make blunders when they set up their opinions in opposition to men—such as Ralph—I will stop before I make a fool of myself.

With the appointed day duly came Lady

Letty, and duly came Marian. The only drawback to the brightness their coming threw over our home atmosphere, lay in one not very important fact. That fact was that, from some mismanagement of myself I concluded, I had contrived to get ill.

Ralph said—but of course he was quite wrong—that he had long known how it must end, and that my illness was the result of my trouble, which he had caused.

Strange! I broke down all at once, like a person who had undergone some great strain upon their powers, of long standing, and had suddenly given way the moment that strain was lifted off.

But that was Dr. Armstrong's explanation, not mine. Dr. Armstrong did not ask me any questions touching the cause of my illness, or I should have disabused his mind at once of any such delusion. But the questions he put to Ralph took a shape having that bearing.

I had no fears for myself. Far otherwise was it, however, with Ralph. He grew dreadfully depressed about me; so much so, that one of my greatest pains consisted in the constant struggle I was of course

obliged to make, to seem well while he was
by, in the face of a weariness nigh unto
death.

That weariness had, like all other appa-
rently unmitigated miseries, its glad and
bright side. Ralph's care of me; his constant watchfulness; his loving tenderness;
his giving up his time to me, reading to me,
drawing me up and down the lawn in my
low bath chair; his carrying me up to bed
at the early hour at which I was obliged
to seek it, and sitting by my side with my
hand clasped in his till I was soothed and
comforted into sleep ;—these things made
sickness almost a blessing to me.

When Lady Letty arrived, I happened
to be on the lawn. As the sound of the
wheels came up, Ralph stopped in the
midst of his labours of dragging my chair
about; and, leaving me a little distance off,
went forward to meet our old friend as she
alighted. This I had begged him to do,
not only out of courtesy to her: I thought
it was quite as well that he should prepare
her a little for the great change she would
find in me, and which might otherwise impress her painfully.

As she approached me, in advance of my

husband, I could see that, in spite of his explanation, she was regarding me very curiously. She had hardly looked that long look in my face, when she turned sharply round to Ralph.

'Why, Colonel,' she said, 'what in the world have you been doing with your wife?'

I answered for him.

'Doing me near to death with kindness, dear Lady Letty,' I said. 'He is the most persevering torment ever sick woman had. I am so glad you are come to keep him in order, and help me to a little more repose. I cannot make him understand that invalids are not able to bear an incessant round of amusements. What with being read to and rolled about, I am half dead.'

Marian now came in for her share of greeting. And soon after, when she and I got shuffled together for a moment by ourselves, Marian whispered to me, 'Don't mind Lady Letty. She is determined to plague you both. Never mind her; she is a little crotchety. I thought I would put you on your guard.'

'What is it about, my dear?' I asked.

'She has got some very uncalled-for notion into her head that you are not happy.'

'Poor dear old soul! I hope that is all she is uneasy about. She will soon find her mistake. Thanks, my dear, thoughtful Marian, for the little hint. It will amuse me much to learn how she got hold of that very quaint crotchet. How do you think Ralph is looking, Marian?'

'Uncommonly well. That curve you used to notice about his mouth is quite gone.'

'Then, my dear, if Lady Letty speaks to you on the subject of my unhappiness, do just ask the poor dear absurd old soul how on earth I could be unhappy, while Ralph is looking, and is really, so remarkably well.'

The meeting between Heine and Marian I thought rather peculiar. All the warmth was on Marian's side.

As for Walter and Ella, we really always thought of them and spoke of them toge- ther, they were such inseparables—they quite appropriated Marian at once. That might possibly account for Heine's so soon retiring into the background after the first natural lover-like embrace.

Lady Letty spared me any allusion to the subject of our odd flight abroad, which

I suppose must have given rise to her suspicion of my unhappiness. She was always
very thoughtful and considerate, and no
doubt supposed the subject would pain me.
But I saw very little of her. Ralph was
obliged to take me away. The talking of
so many people, and the pleasurable excitement of seeing the dear faces again, made
it needful for me very early to beat a retreat.

I insisted on Ralph's leaving me to myself, which he was very loth to do, and
remaining with the party so newly met
together. He obeyed me at last; but left
them all at a very early hour.

'Ah, Ralph,' I said, 'you have broken
up the party on my account, after all I said
to you.'

'No, Grace,' he said; 'I should have
obeyed your injunction to the letter, love,
however much I had longed to come and
comfort you; but the fact is, we are all a
little stiff, somehow. Heine cannot shake
off his depression, even in Marian's presence, and after such a lengthened absence
from her—very sad and unnatural, is it
not? Then of course Marian looks graver
in consequence, than a promised bride

should look in her lover's presence. But
I dare say it is nothing. We shall all
warm up to-morrow. See, darling, I have
brought you a sprig of laurustinus for the
vase on your pet bracket. It is one of the
flexible-branched species, and merits its
name of viburnum, taken from the word
viere, to tie. May it be charmed for you,
my Grace, with some magic of nature
strong enough to tie up anew your poor
little " bundle of life." '

' You have always some pretty device for
my bracket, my Ralph. It was a great
mistake to send you to the wars : you should
have been a poet.'

' Am I not wicked enough as I am?' he
said.

' You are thinking of poor Byron, I
suppose, and others like him? But Ralph,
I think the world makes cruel mistakes in
judging. If men go wrong who have such
divine gifts, in spite of possessing them,
what would they have been without them ?
It is not the poetry that betrays them into
error. The gift does not soil them, but
they the gift. Besides, are other men
better ? Do you not think we should find
men much worse than Byron among those

who could not understand the beauty of
his verse, if only they were, like him,
thrust upon our notice by the mere accident of their popularity. If Mr. Roupe
and Mr. Favrel had been poets, they would
have had a few sins less, perhaps, to answer for, and yet what remained would
have been all set down to the account of
their immortal gift: for they would have
made their vices famous.'

'Grace, I fancy you have hit on a truth.
You think more deeply than I do. I spoke
hastily and foolishly, as I always do. But
I am making you talk too much, my darling.'

'No, Ralph, it refreshes me. Talking to
anyone but you does tire me just now:
but when I am weary, you come upon me
like a breeze.'

'A rough one have I been to you, my
poor, poor broken flower! Oh, Grace, I shall
never forgive myself! It was the shock of
my cruelty. It is that that has broken you
down at last.'

'I told you I was quite happy, Ralph,
except just at the first.'

'I believe you persuaded yourself so,
Grace. A true, noble heart is "deceitful

above all things," but only to itself. You should have been mated to Robert Flemming.'

'I am very partial to Robert Flemming, quite wear him in the deepest of those heart-cells one keeps for one's friends, have often wished I had had such a brother; but you were shaped and fashioned for my needs of soul—you and you only; and to me—save only you—

> All men are shadows,
> Douglas, Douglas, tender and true!

'It is a fit name for me, that of my an-cestor, the " Black Douglas." It used to be a name to frighten children with.'

'Children are easily frightened: I am not a child.'

'Yes you are — in guilelessness and purity. By the way, talking of Robert Flemming, did it never strike you how like he looked sometimes to the St. John of Carlo Dolce?'

'How curious! That is it, then.'

'That is what?'

'I saw once or twice a very peculiarly beautiful expression in his face, like a white light suddenly struck from his eyes, that seemed to flash a moment and fly upward.

It was almost unearthly. Now I remember, he used always vaguely to remind me of some face I had seen before. Of course it was the Carlo Dolce.'

'He did not tell you, I suppose, that I formally made you over to him, in case I had died at Brussels?'

'Good heavens, Ralph!'

'Oh, don't be alarmed; he refused the gift.'

'Ralph! you are a little—just a little, eccentric.'

'So he thought; and so he said.'

'What did he—what could he say?'

'It would be a breach of confidence to tell you that, Grace. Perhaps, however, he will let me tell you some day.'

'Ah! I remember, he said he had reposed some great trust in you, and that you had done the same by him; and he said he would never betray your trust. You are quite right, Ralph, not to betray his. He has a noble heart.'

'A noble heart—a noble, noble heart!'

CHAPTER II.

A MILITARY SUGGESTION.

Ha! ha! here's equity! The dogs
Have as much right as he. But to the issue!

BYRON.

Now I made a vigorous resolve. I determined, if human ingenuity could by any
possible means accomplish it, I would get
myself well.   Here was Lady Letty indulging in all sorts of ridiculous surmises
about us; and the longer I continued in
this unnatural—and for me quite unprece-
dented—state, the worse it would be. Lady
Letty would go wandering about the house,
asking all imaginable questions, and getting
further from the truth with everyone, like
a child playing at 'magic music;' not knowing whether Ralph was 'warm' and I was
'cold' or just the contrary, when the fact
was that we were both now exactly at the
right temperature, and as happy as finches,
and as merry as tomtits.

But just as I was making that magnani-
mous resolution, I got a little worse. That
reminded me of another game played by
the village boys at Easter-tide—the game of
two holding a stick between them for a third
to jump over. Just as the unlucky vaulter
is about to make the leap, the holders thereof
suddenly raise the stick; and, instead of
clearing the barrier, the boy falls on his
back. I took my leap—out of sickness
into health—but the barrier flew up in my
face.

I had nothing for it now, but to keep my
room, see as few faces, and hear as few
tongues as possible, and await a gracious
hand to help me in the next spring I might
dare to take.

Still, though so weak, I was secretly
hugging myself in my seclusion. I had
Ralph all to myself, and I was greedy of
his face, as my mother said May was at
school of her cake and oranges. My desire
—almost my only one now—my desire was
to lie tranced and still like the sleeping lady
in the wood, and listen to the 'magic music'
of the voice I loved. This world had no
music like it to me.

So it happened that all the news nearly

that I came by, came to me through Ralph;
and, though I strongly suspected that on
some points in which I should have felt annoyance had I known all the truth, he cooked
his news to suit my sick state; he was, on
the whole, a very good provider, and gave
me as much as I could well consume.   His
garnishing it was that I relished most, and
when I was more than usually feeble and
inattentive, or failed to grasp and devour
the main contents of the dish, I generally
managed to get hold of the *garnish*—and
I throve upon it!

One piece of news which I had expressed
some anxiety to receive, he did not cook
especially for me—only garnished. He gave
it me just as others had it as far as facts
went, but the little embellishments with
which he edged it round, made it agree
pretty well with me—at least, it did me no
harm; with young meats, sliced lemon is
as medicinal as palatable.

'Do tell me, Ralph,' I said, 'about Heine
and Marian.'

'Oh, there has been the devil to pay!'

That was rather strong garnish.

'I hope you took a receipt in full?' I
said.

'Grace, upon my soul I think you are shamming! There is either nothing the matter with you, or if there be, it is that you are possessed by a spirit of mirth and mischief.'

'Go on; I want to hear.'

'Well, it was a rather serious skirmish, but I think the attacking party has been worsted. Heine, you must know, has been morbidly brooding over one idea,—that it is necessary to his peace of mind to go stark staring mad. He insisted that he was about to commit that folly off-hand, and that it was consequently his duty to live a bachelor all his days, so as to enjoy the visitation 'all alone by himself,' as Lilian used to say when her mother put her in the corner.'

'What did Lady Letty say?'

'A good deal to no purpose.'

'And you?'

'Very little — and quite the contrary. Heine said, "I shall go mad;" and I answered—"Go! go, if you like, by all means; you are making every possible effort to advance yourself on the road. Get there as fast as you can, for I see you are determined. When you arrive at your destination, let us know. *Till* then, we shall make not the slightest alteration in our arrangements." '

' Was Marian told, poor girl? '

' Yes; I went straight to the girl; told her she would have a madman for her husband, and he a wise woman for his wife, and set the two together to argue the point at issue. Never was such an encounter of wits heard!—The women shame us always: she had far the best of the argument. " Heine," she said, laying her true hand on his shoulder and looking straight into his eyes,—" Heine, it is too late to balance chances now. I have thought myself your wife so long, that I shall dare to do a wife's duty by you now, and tell you plainly that you are wrong. There is no such thing as a taint of madness about you, as you say there is. Lady Letty knows more about such things than either you or I do; and she assures me that she has never seen the least sign of it in you. You are fearful on my account, Heine. But I am not afraid. I will hope to make your home so bright to you, Heine, that you will quite forget this unhappy suggestion. Your mind has been much harassed and depressed; but you are

no more mad, or likely to be mad, than
Colonel Elphinstone is."'

'Did you tell Heine that you were——'

'What?' said Ralph, with a start.

'Aware of what Clement Favrel told me.
Should not Heine be told, if he does not
already know it, that Mr. Favrel is not his
father?'

'I think not, Grace.'

'Why, love? what harm could it do?'

'I—I cannot enter into this subject now,
Grace, for the reasons I told you. To give
you a clue to that man's villany would
bring down the whole story upon you at
once. You are not in a condition to endure
it, Grace.'

'Mr. Clement Favrel is still urging you
for sums of money, Ralph. Why do you
let that man prey upon your generosity?'

'How did you know that?'

'Marian was crossing the hall, when he
was let in one day, and she heard him send
in some such message by Stephen as he
once gave to me. Marian entreated me to
warn you against him. She says he is
always speculating and losing his money.
You may as well pour water into a sieve.'

'Grace, my love, you are talking too

much. I shall go down-stairs now, and
come to you again by-and-by. Now, pray,
do not let your little head run on worldly
matters.'

At that moment, there was a knocking at
the door of my room. It was Kitty begging to see how I was. Of course she was
let in; she was my privileged guest whenever she came over from the Glebe. She
always amused me; and she could keep up
such a string of talk as never called for the
exertion of an answer. Ralph remained,
too, after all! He had clearly only desired
to stop my talking and questioning him
about the Favrels, when he threatened to
leave me and go down stairs. How odd!'

' Well, Kitty, how are you getting on at
the Glebe?' he asked.'

' Hearty, thanks to your honour ; hearty,
all matters taken into count.—And, me
lady, how does your honour's self get along?
and you no more but his honour to look to
you.'

' I want no more, Kitty.'

' Ah! me lady, don't I see how it is betwixt the two of ye! Love and sorrow 'll
bring two souls together, if one was at
Jimaiky and t'other here; aye, let 'em alone

to do it, sharp and quick too as the snap of
Mr. Clem Favrel's bull-dogs.'

'Does Mr. Favrel keep bull-dogs, Kitty?'
I asked.

'Don't he, thin, me lady! that's all. And
when they're not particuller busy a-snap-
pin' at people's legs, he keeps the muzzles
of 'em pretty brisk at work a-nuzzlin' at
the ground, a-scratchin' and a tearin' like
mad. And he goes a-diggin' and a-diggin'
hisself from the top of the mornin' to the
bottom of the night, though he doesn't
turn up no petaties worth the mention, and
them only pistol-bullets as he fires down
into the ground after every blessed rain-fall
the Lord sends to make the mould soft for
him to fire into and rattle among the stones,
and any ould kettles and pans there'll may
be buried there, but niver a chest-full of
gold at all, at all.'

'Do you mean to say that he is looking for a treasure, Kitty,?' asked my husband.

'That same, your honour, or somethin'
as like it as Mr. Walter is to your honour;
and if he isn't your honour's own picture,
that other on the wall in the van of me
lady's face was niver painted to match it.'

'That will do, Kitty; I am afraid you
are tiring your mistress.'

'Oh, don't send her away, Ralph.—Has
Mr. Favrel got no servants yet, Kitty?'

'Niver a soul barrin' o' meself, me lady.
And I'll have my hands full anyhow; for
he says he'll have none of 'em, for a pack
o' scamperin', scurryin' hussies not fit to
face a turnip-lantern stuck on a hedge-
stake. But I'll engage he's not been tould
the where I come from, or he'd not be
trustin' a spy in the camp.'

Here Kitty paused, cast her eyes on the
ground thoughtfully, pursed her mouth
and wrinkled up her forehead, as if deep in
the consideration of some knotty question
proposed at a council of war. Suddenly
raising her head at last, she broke out with
the following queer remark:—

'Plase your honour, what a fine post o'
look-out that same Glebe Farm bird-cage
windy 'ud be, if the innimy was drawn up
in line inside o' the Glebe House! That
windy's a-lookin' straight into camp.'

Kitty looked round at my husband as
she made that military suggestion. It
would almost seem as if he were thinking
how to turn her council of war to profit;

for he was lost in a fit of deep meditation.

' That's not a bad idea of yours, Kitty,' he said at last. ' While you hold the key of the position, I think the governor of that fortress might be easily outwitted. But I see your mistress is looking weary. Just go into my study, will you? I have a commission for you.'

Thus was Kitty summarily dismissed. Ralph turned to me before leaving the room.

' My darling,' he said, ' I must leave you awhile. You are not worrying yourself about anything, are you?'

' What, I, Ralph! Surely not. What should I have to worry me? Why, you do not let the shadow of a care come near me!'

' And should such a shadow come near you, should anything surprise or puzzle you, you will leave all—trust all to me—and do me one little service besides.'

' What is that, Ralph?'

' Get well with all the haste you can, my best love!'

' Oh, Ralph, I am trying hard.'

' I know it, love. And to give you a new

spur to help you forward to that longed-for goal of health, let me say one word to you. I want you, Grace; I want your help. There may come that which only a woman's hand can help me in. Your loyal aid, your clear-headed counsel—your loving, pitying heart and noble soul, my own beloved wife, may all be wanting to me. Where should I turn, if not to you?'

'Oh, Ralph, you make me long to be well! If any spur were needed, beyond my wish to be all I used to be to you, you have indeed given it to me now.'

CHAPTER III.

JEST AND EARNEST.

This fellow 's wise enough to play the fool ;
And to do that well, craves a kind of wit :
He must observe their mood on whom he jests,
The quality of persons, and the time ;
And, like the haggard, check at every feather.
Twelfth Night.

So, many
Have hacked their spirit-swords against our fetters,
Broke their great hearts for love, and
Beat out a golden-aged Future from
The angel-metal of their noble lives !
GERALD MASSEY.

THAT spur was a good spur, and the rowel
cut deep! The strong rider who plucked
it from his heel and gave it to me—my
hero, my worthier nineteenth - century
Achilles—knew pretty well what he was
doing when he set the buckle in my hand.
It was as if he had placed his palm beneath
my foot, and cried—'Mount and away!'

In a few days I had left my bed; in a week I was down-stairs.

But though I made so good and effective a start, there was destined to be a new cause why I should yet be somewhat cautious what I was about.

As time rolled on, and before my health could be said to be really much better established—for it will have been seen that I was constantly goading and lashing my feeble powers, and striving to struggle up unnaturally against the sickness which had laid so heavy a hand upon me,—there dawned upon me at once a new hope and a new fear.

I had been awakened to the conviction that I was to be blessed among women; I was looking forward to the day when I should be the sacred mother of a living soul.

Under this new source of inspiration, added to the ' spur ' aforesaid, I was more than ever eager to recover health, and made perhaps rather a too vigorous effort towards that end.

One morning, when I had drawn my workbox to my side, while Ralph was reading, I was plotting quite a long excursion for the following day.

The work I was engaged on was—a little cap; just big enough for a grown-up doll.

It was pretty work, sewing on that miniature border! My fingers seemed to fly over the ground;—but then, no praise to my diligence, it was not that the worker was so nimble, but that the work was so small— oh, so small!

When all was done, the better to judge of the effect, I doubled up my hand into a little round ball, and set the cap on the top of my knuckles—tying the strings under the chin! There, I looked at it, turning my wrist round and round, and fancying to myself how the cap would look with a real little round face in it, instead of my senseless hand.

'Why, you little goose!' cried a voice close to my ear.

' Oh, Ralph,' I said, ' how could you startle me so ! '

' You knew very well I was watching you. When are you going to fit that absurd thing on the right place? When the three ships come sailing in on New-year's Day in the morning? I shall be standing on the quay to see the freight come in.'

' Not so soon as that. But, oh, what a

freight of joy—what a delightful cargo!
A flower of promise, tender and dear, and
sweet in every petal of it!'

'When, then? I am getting impatient.
When the violets take the winds of March
with beauty? Borne on the wings of the
Equinox, eh?'

'More likely, when the violets are tired
of nodding under the bank, and are gone to
sleep with the primroses; and the cowslips
are made into wine; and the wild hyacinth's
bells have rung their last peal on the hare's
track, and lie strewn in the wood-ways; and
the May-blossom's stars are seen no more
among the hay; and the June rose has
fainted upon the hedge thorn; and St.
Swithin objects to being buried under the
chancel-floor, and sends his rains down on
the imbecile monks who would remove him
from the sod where he feels the daisies
growing over him.'

'That will do, Grace; do not let your
mind wander into grave-yards.'

'Ralph,' I said, 'I have just been thinking
that I should like you to drive me to Ap-
pleby. I have all sorts of small purchases
to make, and I really never do get a good
long drive. You are so dreadfully afraid

of my over-exerting myself, that I think by-
and-by you will put me in a glass case.
What was the use of giving me a spur, if I
am not to fly before the wind?'

' Steady — softly, Grace,' he said. ' If
you gallop so fast, you will be out of the
saddle. ·You have a pretty good road before
you, my pearl of riders; but beware of side-
paths and pitfalls. Canter bravely if you
will; but it is a little dark about your way
yet, and you may stumble if you do not let
me guide your rein.'

' I am not riding with " Leonora." '

' God forbid! '

' Nor with the Wild Huntsman.'

' Which of them?—Napoleon?'

' Ralph, I see what you are driving at.
You are for ever trying to keep me from
dwelling upon unpleasant subjects. Do
you really suppose me to be so weak as to
let my mind be affected by bugbears?·How
can you tell me that you find the slightest
resemblance between the wild rider—the
Giant Jäger of the Harz, and the little
Corsican?'

' The greatest resemblance imaginable:
they are identical.'

' What do you mean, Ralph?'

'Just this,—since you will have it. Napoleon—poor conqueror as he was of a world
that slipped from beneath his feet—had
scarcely lifted himself from the outer crust
of this rolling ball of earth, before he was
made to do drill-duty in the air.   He—or
what is left of him—is supposed to hold
splendid reviews at midnight; flags waving,
trumpets blowing, troops marching past in
gallant file, aide-de-camps galloping, princes
looking on;—ay, and princesses such as
you, with little ensnaring knots of hair, mischievous dimples, eyes to win the world—
and me, smiling and extending their white
arms towards him from balconies and "birdcage" windows, ready to pick him off with
all sorts of small explosive ammunition,
where he stands—poor devil! with his back
against a walnut tree, and ready to pounce
upon him the instant he quits its safe shelter,
and hit him with sharp little arrows of
wit;—"hard pounding, gentlemen!" as the
Duke said at Waterloo.'

'Ralph, are you going wild?'

'To be sure; I am off to the hunt directly.
If you want a Wild Huntsman, you must
take me; for, by all the syrens, you shall
have no other!'

' But a review is not a hunt in the air,
Ralph.'

' Not exactly. Napoleon has not reached
so high among the clouds yet: he is on his
way, however. All heroes get up there in
time. In Norway, it is Odin who chases the
wood-spirits, and is to be seen at cock-crow
returning with the little goddesses hanging
to his saddle-bow by their yellow hair. By
the way, if Robert Flemming does not mind,
he will immortalise himself, and catch a
small goddess by her golden hair—and call
her Ella.'

' I wish he would.'

' In Normandy, in the Pyrenees, and
even in Scotland, the huntsman is King
Arthur. Hugh Capet rides near Fon-
tainebleau. At Blois the hunt is called
Chasse Maccabée.'

' Oh, I remember ; and children who die
unbaptized, they fancy, join the rout.'

' That's nonsense : leave the legend to me,
if you please; I have not done yet. In England here, we have caught and caged this
high-flying bird too. In the twelfth century,
we hear of him as the Herlething, or " Erl-
king ; " for, in the reign of our second Harry,
at the head of the airy troop rode the an-

cient British Herla. The scenes of his chase
were the beautiful banks of the soft-flowing
Wye. Gervase of Tilbury gives him to us
again as dropped from the clouds, and en-
joying a delicious full-moon gallop, towards
evening, over British forest and down.'

'My darling Ralph, how can anyone
pretend to be ill where you are? You
would wile the kernel of grief out of the
nut of despair.'

That was Ralph's way. He was certainly
the most many-sided man I ever knew. He
could weep with you, or laugh with you, as
it served your need. He could deal with
solemn things solemnly, yet go wild in
chase of jests. No loaded heart ever appealed to him that it did not become lighter;
no trifler with higher things, but left his
presence cowed by a rebuke. That was my
Ralph.

I was now able to release him a little
from his constant attendance on my wants
and needs. He had even once been to
London—on what business I did not know,
and did not ask. I was happy and content
with everything about me, and only wanted
quietly to get well as quickly as I could,
that I might be of use to Ralph in some

way that he had hinted; what that way was I did not know,—quite, *quite* sure that I, and I only, was to be his helper.

Why do people receive morning visitors? That seems an odd remark to make— a very queer question indeed to tag on to a passage like the above. But if the lines which I had just noted down did suggest that remark, it is clearly no fault of mine—but just a coincidence, or an accident—what you will. What the fact of my hoping to be my husband's helper under his difficulties, I, and I only, had to do with Mrs. Burlington's call, the poor souls in Bedlam alone could solve.

By the way—no. Mrs. Burlington's visit is clearly an anachronism here. It must be postponed.

Well, then, let me speak of Lady Letty. There is a repose about Lady Letty, a comfort in her presence, which no Mrs. Burlington ever could bring with her, or ever did. Mrs. Burlington again! Why am I thinking of Mrs. Burlington?

'Grace,' said Letty, 'I am going to leave you for awhile. I do not feel as if I were in my right place, somehow.'

'Lady Letty,' I cried in amazement, 'are you not happy with us?'

'Quite happy, my dear,' she replied, 'but a little out of my element, somehow. I can hardly tell what it is that makes me say so; but I think it has been my own fault. Have you not lately avoided me a little, Grace?'

'Dear Lady Letty!'

'Well, my dear, I told you it was my fault. I suppose you read it all in my eyes —that I have been a foolish old woman; that, in short, I got it into my head, soon after your return to Fairfield, that you and your husband had been on bad terms, and that that was why you had gone off to Waterloo—to fight it out on the old battle-field. The fact is, I have heard a good deal about you both, my dear, since you came back. You know, Dr. Percy is a great correspondent of mine—almost as constant a one as Mrs. Armstrong.'

'Mrs. Armstrong!' I could not help exclaiming.

'Yes, my dear. If it had been the doctor—Dr. Armstrong himself, I hope there would have been no impropriety. He is a steady-going married man, you know, and I am decidedly out of my teens. I shall

be out of my *tys* some day, if I keep as
hearty as I have been since I went to Scar-
borough. Only think, if I should live to
be a hundred! What tough hearts single
women must have! Here am I, and nothing
touches me; here were you almost at
death's door for some stupid misunderstanding.'

'What, Lady Letty?' I said.

'Oh, my dear, never mind my knowing.
The truth is, that Mrs. Armstrong told me.'

'Told you what, Lady Letty?' I asked;
for I was too old a soldier to do anything
but express the most lying surprise at the
idea of a misunderstanding between Ralph
and me. My face would perhaps have betrayed me, but that I was most genuinely
surprised; could not conjecture how it was
possible that she could have learned it—
Mrs. Armstrong, I mean.

'Why, my dear, about your sleep-walking
and its unfortunate cause.'

'Mrs. Armstrong must have made some
mistake,' I said.

'Doctors never make mistakes, my dear.
Dr. Armstrong had it from your husband,
and she had it from hers.'

'What, the sleep-walking, Lady Letty!'

I replied, laughing. 'He must have caught
that from me, if he caught it from either
of us; for it was I that walked, not Ralph.
Are you not aware that I was a sleep-walker
when a child?'

'No, my dear! Is that true, child? Mrs.
Armstrong may have been mistaken, certainly. But then there is your husband's
confession to hers.'

'Confession of what, Lady Letty?'

'That he had been most unkind to you.'

'Lady Letty, you astound me! Do not
mistake me; I am not in the least astounded
that my husband should say that of himself; but I own I am surprised that you
should not know him better, after knowing
him so long.'

'Why, he is not in the habit of telling
fibs, is he, my dear?'

'Do not trouble yourself to wrap them
up in that pretty delicate way, as if you
were speaking of a little child's lapse from
truth, Lady Letty. I can bear to hear the
word, because I am quite used to the thing.
And I thought you knew Ralph's one pecu-
liarity. You know, you used to admit,
before I married him, that he was very
peculiar. Whenever he is speaking of him-

self and his failings, he certainly does " lie
like truth, and yet most truly lie." '

'Oh, you mean to say that he has been
romancing.'

'That's exactly it, Lady Letty. And
now will you please to allow me to order
the carriage for you?'

'Grace! are you going to turn out an
old friend from your door in that manner?'

' Will you allow me to order the carriage
for you, Lady Letty?'

' No, Grace, I will not be indebted to you
for the use of your carriage. I shall go by
the coach.'

' The coach does not run till the morning——'

' Then I will sleep at the Lodge.'

' Will you, if you please, Lady Letty, if
you are not in a hurry to go to the Lodge,
allow me to finish my sentence?'

'I thought you had finished it, Grace!
I thought you were really quite angry—
though I cannot say you looked so—quite
angry at what I had been saying, and were
positively going to turn me out.'

' What was there to be angry about, Lady
Letty?'

' Why, my dear, when people go about

telling stories of this sort that are not true, it is very annoying.'

'Not the least. If my husband were unkind to me, I dare say I should not like to hear it talked about, and should be nettled at being told of it; but, as it is, it is scarcely worth a smile—and that is really all I can give to it. What I was going to say was, will you allow me to order the carriage for a little drive for you? Lilian will be glad to see you, especially as you think of being so unkind as to desert us. And as you will have plenty of time before you return to dinner, you can, if you like, you know, say your farewells to the Armstrongs. Poor Mrs. Armstrong! I think it might do her good.'

'What, the sight of my old phiz, my dear?'

'No, dear, kind Lady Letty, not that; though it is as pleasant a face as I know, —except one. I meant that your good sense, your admirable manner of giving good advice, might be the saving of that woman.'

'I must be very dull, Grace; but upon my life, my dear, I do not take your meaning.'

'Only this, Lady Letty—you know that

when a wife has her husband's fullest confidence, and in his most unguarded moments
draws the thoughts of his heart into her
own, it is but a little thing he asks of her,
if he asks her to keep the counsel he shares
with her, and not rise up and tender to
another the trust he left sleeping when he
rose and quitted her side. A woman who
does so, Lady Letty, to my thinking does
almost as cruel a wrong to her husband as
if she went and gave the kiss he left upon
her lips to the keeping of a stranger.'

'My dear, you are perfectly right: you
astonish me.'

'Do I do so much wrong, Lady Letty, as
to make it a matter of surprise that I
should be right for once?' I asked, smiling.

'I am not astonished at you, my dear,
but at myself. I am so much older than
you are, and yet I never thought of that;
and at my years it is left for you to teach
me. I am ashamed of myself — fairly
ashamed of myself, my dear.'

'It is not your fault, Lady Letty; only
your sorrow, dear old friend! You never
knew the sweetness of wifehood.'

'Ah! that is it, I suppose. Well, my
dear, I suppose we have quite made it up

now. Still, I—I think, my dear, I shall return to Hollywood.'

' Oh, why, dear, dear Lady Letty?'

' Why, the fact is, my dear, that, old as I am, I positively cannot endure the sight of your happiness: I really cannot, my dear. It fills my old heart with all sorts of longings, that I ought to have packed up in my coffin more than a quarter of a century ago, ready to take to the other world with me. I could curse my stars, or dash my old head against the wall, or do any other mountebank trick, only just to look at you. I feel as if all my youthful feelings, nailed and hammered down for twenty years, were bursting their sepulchre and making life hideous with their ghosts. It makes me as mad as Clement Favrel, when I think of his brother Leonard, and all the tender hopes and selfless wishes I twined about that man. If I stay here, I positively must live totally apart in some out-of-the-way corner of the house.'

And Lady Letty laughed—a sore laugh —till she cried.

' I cannot laugh, Lady Letty,' I said.

' No my dear, I am sure you cannot. It

is no laughing matter, Grace: though men would split their sides to hear me.'

'Not Ralph.'

'Yes, he would, my dear; to hear me talk so,—me, with my fifty years, and my old changed face, and my poor graceless figure, and my fat clumsy arms, and my mapped hands, with all life's rivers marked out upon them, and my scant grey hairs, and my expressionless lips, and my eyes with little bags under them, to weep tears over my lost youth in. Oh! child, child, what an old fool I am!'

'God's wisdom knows better, Lady Letty.'

'Oh, my dear, I have sometimes dared to cry out against His way of ordering the world: that was long ago, in my misery— not now. Yet you see, my dear, my blank of life was all of my own making. He who has given me peace in my old age, would have filled up that blank for me, if I had not, like a froward child, beaten against His hand. I might have married Leonard, and been as happy as you are. But I was stilted and romantic. You know something of how it was I came to run

away from Leonard. I told that story
briefly, for the Colonel and Heine were
present, and they could not have understood my feelings in the matter: but, do
you know, Grace, what I felt was the sort of
incongruity of marrying Leonard under
those conditions—his not caring for me,
but only my money, as I was led to believe.
People say a good deal that is unkind
against a woman who weds a man whom
she does not love in a determined manner;
but I think they are harsh and wrong—
unless, indeed, the woman is led by merce-
nary considerations. Many a young creature with a wrecked heart, which she has
broken asunder upon some flinty rock of a
fellow, will turn with tenderness to a man
who loves her worthily—or seems to do so,
and for his sake will be willing to forget
self once more in a new dream of devoted-
ness. But, oh! my dear child, just imagine
what it must be to be the wife of the man
you love with all your heart and soul,
knowing all the while that he cares nothing
in the world for you! Just think of its
coming to pass that he should one day tell
you, his wife, to your face, that you had
married him, caring nothing about his hap-

piness. Only fancy, now, Leonard saying to me, "There, now, Lætitia, you have plotted and succeeded. You loved me with a selfish love. I cannot respect you. You have wrecked my life, and I curse the hour when I was born, and doubly curse the hour when first I met you."'

'Dreadful! But, oh! dear Lady Letty, what a sad mistake it was!'

'Ah! it was indeed, my dear. But it just serves to show us how weak we are when we take the ruling of our life into our own hands. It could not be helped. I had no guidance but my own judgment: I suppose I had not prayed heartily enough for guidance from above. As it was, I made a cruel mistake, to my Leonard's undoing and my own.'

'The sin was Clement Favrel's, and not yours, Lady Letty.'

'Well, yes, he was the pivot that turned the unlucky wheel of my destiny, my dear. He is a bad man, and I do not think he had done all the mischief he was permitted to do in this world, when he set me rolling the wrong way on the road of life. Does it not strike you, my dear, that those boys he gives his name to are not one bit like him?

Do you know, I begin to suspect they are not his sons after all.'

'Heine, I have often thought, is too strictly true and honourable to be the son of such a worthless father,' I said; but I did not think it well to tell Lady Letty even, as she was so much with Marian, that I knew the boys were not Clement Favrel's sons; because my husband had said he thought it best that the fact should not come to their ears. 'As for Walter,' I added, ' he is even less like him in every way. Walter is the image of Ralph.'

' That struck me very particularly, the moment I saw him. It is lucky we know all about the Colonel's former life,' she added, smiling, ' or we should have been inclined to imagine there had been some fair Rosamond in the case, with all the romantic additions of the silken clue, and the bower in a wood, and the key in the Colonel's pocket, side by side with the key of the Glebe Farm, which he keeps in that absurd locked-up manner. Mrs. Burlington asked me the other day, by the way, if he could be persuaded to let her have a peep into that " blue chamber" of horrors; but I put her off, for I know he hates making a show-place of the Glebe Farm, or anything belonging to it.'

'What possible motive could the man have—Clement Favrel, I mean—for passing these youths off as his own children, if they are not so, and keeping the knowledge of their real parentage from them, do you think?'

'Heaven only knows, my dear; but he is capable of any iniquity, I really do believe. God forgive me if I have misjudged the man! He may have murdered their father, for what we know. Or they may be the children of some nobleman; and Clement Favrel has found it answer his purpose to take charge of them: he seems to get large sums of money every now and then to speculate with. Perhaps that is their father's hush-money.'

'What, Lady Letty! Say that again.'

'Don't you know what I mean by hush-money, my dear? People call by that name, money which is given to keep a transaction secret. The father of these boys—especially if he is now a married man—would be liberal, no doubt, to a man who could blab if he chose.'

'I see, Lady Letty,' I said.—Why did I catch my breath and gasp?

'Depend on it, my dear, there is some disgrace attaching to their birth. I have long suspected it; but of course I have not said anything to Marian about it, as it is all a vague conjecture. But you must have noticed that Heine always calls the man "Clement Favrel," and never his "father."'

'I see, Lady Letty.'

'I almost think the Colonel knows something more about them than he chooses to say; he is so kind, so affectionate to them. But he will never betray it, if he does. You might tear the Colonel piecemeal before he would utter one word to wound a human being—and it might injure their mother, perhaps.'

'I see—I see, Lady Letty.'

CHAPTER IV.

THE MAGPIE'S NEST.

Who is the happy Warrior? * * *
It is the generous spirit who, when brought
Among the tasks of real life, hath wrought
Upon the plan that pleased his childish thought;
Whose high endeavours are an inward light
That make the path before him always bright:
* * * Who, if he be called upon to face
Some awful moment to which Heaven has joined
Great issues, good or bad for human kind,
Is happy as a Lover; and attired
With sudden brightness, like a Man inspired.

Wordsworth's Happy Warrior.

LADY LETTY was not permitted by us to leave our fireside in that summary manner. But she did so before many months were over. Then she took with her Marian, and Heine as well.

Nothing would induce Marian to leave her lover any more. She was perfectly right; and she was as straightforward and

as firm in the matter as might have been
expected of a girl of her noble nature.

'No, Lilian,' she said, one day when the
Rectory party had come up to dine with us
previous to our old friends leaving us, 'I
will never quit Heine's side any more. He
is in a sadly depressed condition of mind;
but I feel sure he will come all right if he
is left to me. I am not so very sensitive as
he is just now, and he says he is always
better when we are left quite to ourselves.
By-and-by, no doubt, our relative positions
will be reversed. He will be my guide, and
I shall lean on him. Just now I know
how to comfort and cheer him; and nothing
shall induce me to desert him for one
moment.'

So it was finally settled that the lovers
should proceed with Lady Letty to Hollywood, have the run of those fair lawns and
woods, and make themselves happy their
own way.

Lady Letty was full of apologies to me
for deserting me at such a time—for I was
now not very far from my confinement.

'I really am ashamed to leave you, my
dear,' she said, 'but what am I to do? I
can be of no possible use to you; for what

use can an old-maid be to a young mother?
And besides, do you know I should feel so
dreadfully unnerved and uncomfortable,
and so should make everybody in the house
unnerved and uncomfortable too? I could
not bear to hear the baby cry. That is a
sound I never could endure. My milkless
breast is torn by it; it makes all my blood
weep. All that should have been motherhood within me becomes a strain of agony.
The little babe's mouth seems to pout to
me, the little hands to tear my dress open,
the little legs to be crawling, crawling to my
heart's very core. I am not going to endure
it, my dear, I can tell you. If I were
younger, I could battle with my feelings,
as I used to battle; I am too old for that
now: my nerves and my pulses do not
obey the rein of my will nearly so well as
they used to do. I shall come and see you
some day, when the queer little creature is
weaned, and has become like any other
tumbling animal; then I can look at it
more quietly as it sprawls on the grass.—
I would rather not face it with the mother's
milk in its mouth.'

So the house was almost empty again;
there was only Ella left to me. Walter

had returned to Clement Favrel's house, the Glebe House, after their visit to us long ago, as well as Heine. Now that Heine was gone to Hollywood with Marian and Lady Letty, Walter was very lonely there, and came a good deal to us. Lilian, Lawrence, and Dr. Percy were, of course, much with us. Beyond these, we—or, at least, I—saw very few guests. Ralph dined out sometimes, but never when he could decently get out of it. And so we lived our quiet home-life up to the time, now so close at hand, when I looked—oh, blessing of blessings!—to hold my treasure in my arms.

It had happened, very unfortunately, that I had never regained the strength I might reasonably have hoped to regain. I could not account for it—neither could anyone else: but so it was. I grieved over the deprivation secretly; but I kept my trouble from my husband. Once or twice I had told him that I felt quite sufficiently recovered to make myself useful to him in that matter he had slightly referred to, as one in which I could serve him greatly. But he seemed to think otherwise. He always said that there was now no hurry about it: he even admitted once—I think unintentionally—that he *had* some help now. Who could that be: Kitty? It *could* be no one else.

I was at this time able to take short walks with Ralph, just about the pleasure-grounds: I never went beyond them. Leaning on his arm, I enjoyed these rambles greatly; and he seemed never weary of supporting me, though it must have been very tiresome and very cramping to his limbs to walk at my slow pace. Then, too, it was trying in another way. If he could have walked quite upright, it might not have been so fatiguing to him: but he would always make me walk with his arm round my waist for my more complete support, after the first few paces; and he being so much taller than I was, was obliged to walk in a half-stooping position. I often begged him to give me his arm again.

'Why, Grace, what do you think a man was made for?' he would say. 'You were created for my blessing—especially for me, you know. And if I am not very much mistaken, I was meant to be your support —your stake, your staff, your great tall

F 2

leaning-post.   That was why no "bullet"
ever "found its billet" in my long shanks.'

'You were wounded in the leg, too,
Ralph,' I said one day when he made that
remark, as we were walking.

'A mere scratch—just enough to call my
attention to the fact that I had a pair of
long legs for your service, to roll you about
in wheeled chairs, and trot you out when
these delicate little limbs of yours want the
other pair to help them along.'

'Do you remember the illness you had
when that old wound broke out afresh—
when you were so depressed in mind?'

'Quite well.—But do not let us talk of
old wounds.   They are all healed now.'

'It may break out again.'

'Not the least likely.   I feel as whole
and hearty as ever I was in my life.   Why,
I feel as young again as I did a year ago.'

'What has made such a change in you,
Ralph?   Your spirits lately have been like
a boy's.   I scarcely know you.'

'I am a boy—a perfect urchin of a boy,
Grace. — You ask me what makes me
so?   Well, several things, I think.   I hope
I am of some small use to you; that is
one item to be taken into the account.

And then I have a sort of idea that I have
a little lady in a woodland bower, that loves
the arms she nestles in, like a broken-winged
dove.'

'In a woodland bower?'

'This is all one pleasant bower, is it not—
smooth velvet lawn, pleached alley, orchard,
shrubbery, wood, dingle, moor, and wild?
Is there any spot of it all that is not hallowed by some dear and fond recollection?
Shall I ever forget the footsteps on the
Elphin's Stone, or the kiss under the clear
sky, beneath the March tassels of the early
birch? Shall I ever lose from my ear the
voice of the nightingale that sang our first
bridal song when we returned to Fairfield?
Shall I ever see so beautiful a sight anywhere as the skir of the plover over our
heads, as we lay dreaming in among the
heath-patches and wild-thyme, in what the
Scotch so prettily call the hour of the
" gloaming?" Or the light of a certain face
—the face of one who found me lost among
the snows on " Herrick's Ridge," and held
her breast to mine to warm me into life?
Or the hand of the horsewoman who snatched
me out of the tiger's jaws on the road to
" Hitchen's Copse?" '

' Ralph ! '

' Well, darling? '

' I think I can tell what it is that makes you so glad and happy just now—just now, when I am so feeble and so entirely unable to echo your pleasant mood of mirth and mischief—almost too feeble to follow it, or enjoy it.'

' Well, what do you think it is—if you will not take my word for it that you are the cause,—part of the cause, at any rate?'

' I will tell you. I think, Ralph, you must have been doing some particularly good action ; something greater and higher —nearer to God, in short—than your usual acts; and to me they all seem good, and great, and wise, and kind.'

' Why, you little flattering soul! Grace, my little spoiler, what put that idea into your head? I thought you looked all this day as if there was something on your mind; as if you were striving to solve some knotty problem, and did not choose to let me help you in the working of it. So, that is the little magpie's egg you have hatched, is it?'

' Yes, Ralph, I feel quite sure of it now. I have been a littled puzzled by one or two things; and that is the conclusion I have come to.'

'A very fair and kind conclusion, too. And if it satisfies you as well as if it were a truth,—well! then it is just as good as the truth to you, you know.'

'I do not think that remark of yours, Ralph, was quite a right one, somehow.'

'What is there wrong about it ?'

'Nothing that is not truth can supply the place of truth, Ralph.'

'Well, perhaps not. If we are to draw morals out of every random word we say, as the talkers do in a wrong-headed, stupid, ill-written child's book, I grant I spoke amiss. All I meant was, my love, that any kind thought of me that had found its way into the hollow of your breast—like a silver spoon in a magpie's nest—might very well rest there for awhile, just till the little nestling is safely hatched. Then, I dare say, it will be tossed out by the small hungry beak as good for nothing whatever.'

'Oh!'

'Why do you start ? What are you looking at ? Do you see anything amiss about my dress? Oh! What does that

mean? The magpie does not sing—
Oh!'

'Ralph, where were you this afternoon,
before you came in to take me for a walk?'

'Up at the Glebe Farm, Grace.'

'Alone, Ralph?'

'No, Grace.'

'Was Kitty there, then?'

'No, Grace.'

'Oh!'

'Upon my word, I never heard such a
magpie in all my life!'

'Had you been walking under the trees,
Ralph?'

'Yes. I walked down by the row of trees
that skirt the clover-meadow first, for I
had to speak to Thornley about some farming matters, and I saw him standing there
as I was on my way to the Glebe Farm.
Why do you ask?'

'I thought you had,—I thought you had
been walking under the trees,—that's all.'

'Why did you think I had?'

'Because—because—because the old last
year's nests of the magpies are breaking
away from the boughs;—the rains have come
down from heaven, and the flood has broken
over them;—the down and feathers that

lined the nest are scattered and strewed by the rough wind;—and the twigs that bound the nest to the bough-shelter are snapped and broken;—and the binding and lapping of the leaves is no more,—and—and—and—

The flowers of the forest are a' wede away!'

'Grace, don't sing!—pray, don't sing with that voice! I really do not know your voice: I never heard such a sound in my life: it harrows my very soul. Grace—Grace, for Heaven's sake tell me, is anything the matter? Are you ill?—are you worse?'

'My head—my head!'

'I *knew* you were ill.'

'Take me in.'

'I will, my darling. Have you any pain besides that in your head?'

'Yes, a little.'

'Where?'

'At my heart.'

'Come! I will carry you. See, now here we are at home again almost.—Hang this infernal gate; there is no getting it open!—There, now we are through at last; we shall be home in a minute.'

'Set me down here—here, at the door: I can walk upstairs quite well. I do not want anyone to help me.'

'Better let me carry you up.'

'No, pray don't.'

'Let me just guide you up the stairs; you are tottering.'

'I can walk.'

'Stay, love; here is something of yours that has dropped out of the breast of my waistcoat. Had you a blue ribbon in your dress?'

'No—no; it is not mine.'

'Then how, in the name of Heaven, did it come here?'

'Out of the trees—the trees you passed under on your way to the Glebe Farm; or —no, as you came back,—as you came back, you know.'

'But where could it have come from? The silk-worms do not breed there; and if they did they do not weave their own silk into blue velvet ribbons. Where *could* it have come from?'

'The magpie's nest!'

CHAPTER V.

A PAINTED JEZEBEL.

What did the wanton say ?   *   *
They judge all Nature from her feet of clay,
Without the will to lift their eyes, and see
Her godlike head crowned with spiritual fire,
And touching other worlds.—I am weary of her.
ALFRED TENNYSON.

I WENT upstairs into my dressing-room.
I was alone; for I had put from me the
hand that would have comforted me best
at any other time: not now—not now!
That hand had been used to bathe my
temples when they ached, but now I must
do it myself or leave it undone; or I could
summon a servant, or Ella would do it.   O
yes, anybody could come and look in my
eyes, and see how wild they were, and read
there——Oh, of course.

It was likely, was it not, that I should
ring the bell?

I sat down by the window, with my head
on my hand. Was I thinking? I doubt:
no, I was gasping a little—that was all.
Ah! yes; I was doing one other thing. I
was measuring with a curious eye the height
of the window from the ground; speculating
in fancy as to how anyone might manage
just to mount to the sill, and take a little
leap from that point of vantage; and whether
it would prove effectual; and who would
find the body; and where the inquest would
be held, in the study below or at the village
inn? I was curious, too, in imagining how
Mr. Sheringham would be affected at the
inquest: I thought I could see him throwing
his handkerchief from hand to hand, and
looking steadily at the game,—not seeing
at all the ball into which he had rolled that
handkerchief, for something that swam in
his eyes. Yes, and he would be chief
mourner, too. Would there be any other?
O dear, no—not likely—not likely at all;
too busy, up at the Glebe Farm; 'could not
possibly attend.'

There was salt of sorrel in yonder drawer:
would that be better? It had some of it
been used for taking out stains. There
was yet a little left. Would there be enough

to wash out life? It was deep engrained: we were all long livers, we Harcourts— yes, my name was Harcourt—yes, of course it was Harcourt.

I would rise and find it. The drawer is stiff. Am I going to let that baulk me? What folly! It *shall* open.——There, now I have it. There seems to be enough.—A glass and water? They are both at hand. Happy chance—happy deliverance!

What is it that arrests my hand? What am I about to do? Am I mad? Did God give me life, or am I only dreaming that I live? What holds me back? Why do I not drink and die? Is it my own life alone against which my wild impious hand is raised, or is it against another's too?—True: there *is* another life. What am I about to do with that?—Murder—murder!——My God! my God!

*　　*　　*　　*　　*

I have a faint recollection of having been lifted from the floor; a dim dreamy memory of wishing to wander away—I knew not, cared not whither; was conscious of seeing some one, who must have been waiting and watching outside the door. It was Colonel Elphinstone, I thought, the hero of Waterloo.

Yes, it was he.   It was very kind of him.
He carried me in and laid me on my bed.

He went away very soon.   I could be no
companion for him.   How could I talk to him
of sieges and battles, and trenches and on-
slaughts and artillery, and all the pomp and
circumstance of glorious war?   Out of the
question,—quite.

Now I think of it, it is not he, but
Kitty.—I am perplexed, Kitty, that is all:
a little confused, you see; cannot at all get
at the truth of it.

What drink are you giving me, Dr. Armstrong?   I hope your wife is well?   But
pray, tell her not to repeat what you say
to her.   It was quite false; he is kind, very,
very kind to me.

Thank you, love; I will go to sleep now.

 * * * * *

‘ Have I slept long, Kitty?   My head is
quite clear now.   What have I been saying,
Kitty?’

‘ Only a-ramblin’ a bit, me lady, about a
thing you couldn’t make out anyhow.
That’s the very way with us all when the
sickness is upon us.   It’s just like the night-
mare that comes of lying on our backs,
when everything’s a trouble to us; and it’s

all mad bulls and no tree to climb, and the gate barred, and the dogs chained up when they ought to be loosed; or the man that's stole our purse is on before us a-flyin' like the wind away with the gould our grandmother left us to wake her with before the banshee had done wailin', and its all flintstones under our feet, and ropes acrost the road, and we a-stumblin' and a-trippin' of our heels and pattens, and no way made after him no more than if we'd stayed at the startin'-post a-weavin' of gossamers for nets to catch the moon with. Or it's a-tumblin' off of a precipice we are, and comin' down on our own bed—plump! And it's many a queer thing there is in our waking, too, me lady, that we can't make out neither. There's many a close thing that is a hard nut to crack; and when you've cracked it, maybe you'll find there's nothin' in it at all, at all, and only your teeth the worse for your trouble. But things all comes round in time, just like a mill-horse, and the miller no trouble in life, but just to stand by and bide his time. And when your head's cut open with a sabre-cut, though things look ugly, the army-surgeon 'll sew it up in no time and less; and by-and-by, as sure as

cure, there's only the scar of the gash left all
hard and dry, and the hair growin' over
and over it, till not a man in the regiment
ud ever drame you'd been slashed at, and
you don't remember it yourself.'

'I will get up now, Kitty; I feel quite
myself again.'

'You are bether in your bed, me lady.'

'No; I prefer to get up.'

'Then it's not I'll hinder ye, me darlin'.
But glad I'll be to see you look so bright
again, and the masther a-comin' in, may be.'

'Where is he, Kitty?—No—no; I did
not mean to ask you to tell me where he
is; I will ask him myself. He will tell me
all I want to know; but I do not want to
know anything. Mr. Armstrong has been
here, has he not?'

'That's what he has, me lady. When
me masther found ye lyin' on the floor—for
he'd waited outside till he heard ye fall—
when he picked ye off the floor, he laid
ye down in your bed as soft as if ye'd been
a two-months baby; and he sent off man
and horse for the doctorin' man, and he
gave you a drink that set ye to sleep; and
I come up in the nick o' the time, and kept
me post by your bed; and then the masther

went out when he was tould you'd only been over-walkin' of yourself, and you'd come all right after a slape.'

I did get up. I was myself again—such as that was. I went downstairs; and was surprised by a visitor.

When Mrs. Burlington was announced, I was sitting with Ella in a room which had been set apart for her as her own private snuggery, and she was engaged in reading to me.

As I rose up to seek the reception-room where this most unwelcome visitor awaited me, Ella was about to follow.

'No, dear Ella,' I said, 'you must not go with me.'

' Why, dear Mrs. Elphinstone?'

' I will tell you, Ella,' I answered. ' Any other guest who comes to the Grange I am glad for you to see, only not this Mrs. Burlington. I cannot exactly say what there is about her that I so dislike, but I have a sort of instinctive feeling that she is not the kind of person I should like to see you associate with. That is all, Ella. So, please, wait here for me; she will not stay long, I dare say.'

'But,' said Ella, hesitating, 'I would rather go with you—please let me.'

'Indeed, Ella, I cannot. Why do you urge it, my love?'

'Because— because, dear Mrs. Elphinstone, I—I would rather go where you go.'

In a moment I divined what this meant. Ella had been set to watch me—not to lose sight of me lest I should come to harm.

'Ella,' I said, 'you have been told not to leave me for a moment.'

Ella could not lie with her eyes any more than with her tongue. She saw that I knew she was my guardian and jailer for the time being.

'Pray let me go with you,' she said; 'you might be ill again, and—and, indeed, indeed if I were to leave you before Colonel Elphinstone comes home, I should feel that it was a breach of trust.'

'And I, dear Ella, should feel it a breach of trust to our dear friend Robert Flemming if I were to permit you to associate with any but the good and pure—as he is good and pure. So yield to me, my sweet Ella. Indeed, dear, I am quite myself again. And as for my husband's charge to you to keep me in view, leave me to make your peace with him.'

So I overruled, kissed, and left her.

What a time for a call! Why it was five o'clock.

As I opened the door of the drawing-room, and faced her, the whole volume of the woman burst upon me at once. Neither inborn grace nor its poor substitute, polish, was hers. Her very dress seemed not to rustle, but to crackle : like its wearer it had neither softness, nor that lustre which appears to give more light than it receives, making much of a little ray because of the richness which is its own. She rose up with a heave, and swept down upon me like an avalanche.

To record her speech is next to impossible. When she uttered platitudes, her voice was loud and harsh. When she wished to imply more than she knew she dared to utter, she sank her voice to a whisper that was something like the hissing of a serpent.

' How do you do?—well? *Quite* well, I hope, my *dear* Mrs. Elphinstone ? I want just *five* minutes' conversation with you. *Have* you bespoken a nurse ?—I do

not mean a monthly nurse; that sort of
person you have no doubt engaged. But
if you want an entirely unexceptionable
young person to take the child from the
month, I think I could lay my hand at this
moment on the proper party.'

'Thank you; I have no doubt you could,
but I am provided.'

'A Fairfield young person?'

'Yes; I intend to be my own nurse, Mrs.
Burlington.'

'Dear me! the Colonel will not like that;
the men hate to see the brats always
dangling at a woman's knee.'

'The Colonel is not one of "the men"
of that kind; he would like to see a dozen
all clinging about me at once, I believe.'

'*I* think a husband ought to claim a
wife's undivided attention.'

'Well now, do you know, I do not. I
am afraid your nature is a little—just a
little sophisticated. The birds are my
teachers. The male bird feeds his mate
while she is busied with her young, sings
to her to lighten her labours, takes a good
share of the toil, and with her, too, teaches
the young to fly, when their time is full
and the woods want them.'

' The noisy callow things! I can assure you, from my own experience, that the men do not like their rest to be disturbed by the uproar of children. *My* husband could not bear them.'

' Your husband reminds me of a little Esquimaux——'

' A little Esquimaux!'

' Yes, a little Esquimaux that our friend Major Cartright told us of the other day. The poor little soul had lived so long on blubber and whale-oil stuffed down his throat by his wife, that he was quite unfit for a more civilised life when he found himself among us better-dieted men and women. All he could say was " Too much noise, too much people, too much house: Oh for Labrador!" '

' I dare say I am very obtuse, but really now I don't see your analogy. By the way, do you remember a Mr. Roupe whom we met—you and I, you know, at Mr. Sheringham's some little time ago?'

' Yes, quite well.'

' Do you know, my dear, I think he admired you very much?'

' Madam!'

'Oh! pray don't lift your eyebrows in that

strange manner—though really they are
very pretty eyebrows; I don't at all
wonder at the men admiring them. Mine
were just like that at one time, quite like
little pencil-lines. Do not think me vain.
I am not giving my own opinion; but I
was told so by a rising young artist — a
very handsome languishing looking youth
he was—who came to paint Burlington's
portrait—he *would* paint mine too—and
it was he that told me my eyebrows were
quite beautiful—enough to make a man die
for love. He said they looked just as if he
had made them with one curving sweep of
his brush. And "*Might* he try?" he asked.
And do you know the saucy young fellow
took his brush—it was one day when Burlington was out; *he* might not have liked
it, you know—the saucy young fellow had
the impertinence, *actually* the impertinence,
do you know, to take his brush, with real
nasty oil-paint in it, and pass it over both
my eyebrows. Odd creature! I suppose
he was vexed to find that he could not
come up to nature; for, do you know, he
threw down his brush in disgust, and turned
away with quite a curl of his lip. But,
dear me, I see I am taking up your time,

dear Mrs. Elphinstone. I always know when my hostess rises from her seat and walks to the window that she is looking out to see if my coachman is not tired of waiting. Ha! ha! ha! That's quick of me, isn't it?'

'Mrs. Burlington, your horses are shivering.'

'Oh no! thank you, though, for being so careful of my cattle. But it is only a skin-shiver; it is the horse-fly stinging them. As I was saying—let me see, where was I?— Oh! about the young person, you know——'

'Mrs. Burlington, your coachman is nodding.'

'Oh! is he? Well, good evening. But, pardon me one moment—have you heard the last little bit of village gossip? *You* ought to know all about it; but I suppose the story has been carefully kept from your ears for fear of alarming consequences. Do you know that there *is* a report going abroad that the Glebe Farm ghost is walking again? has been seen standing just exactly where it used to stand at that old "bird-cage" window, with the ivy and the clematis and all that green stuff about it, you know. And they *do* say it is the very identical

image, only older, you know—I suppose
ghosts grow like other people, don't they?—
the very identical image of the ghost that
used to frighten the farmers' boys nearly
twenty years ago! It is quite an alluring
face, I'm told, with a pretty little fillet round
its head—a blue snood, in short. I say, my
dear, the Colonel keeps the key of the Glebe
Farm, does he not? I wonder he doesn't
pull the horrid old place down. But perhaps he has a fancy for pretty alluring
ghosts with charming little becoming blue
fillets round their heads? Ha! ha! ha!'

' Good evening, Mrs. Burlington.'

' Oh! good evening, good evening—*good
evening.*'

CHAPTER VI.

THE OBSERVATORY.

He stands,
One of those fair and visioned forms
That, like the rainbow, come in storms,
And bear through more than mortal strife
The treasure of a charmèd life!
Upon his brow the grace revealed
Which kings have stamped, and Gods have sealed;
He rises on her in the night
Like some bright spirit of the sea,
And stands before her in the light
Of his own high nobility!

T. K. HERVEY.

ONE, two, three, four, five, six. Why, it was six o'clock! In another hour the dinner bell would ring: Ralph would be home—home!

How should I meet him? 'With smiles,' says that grim liar, the world: at all times and seasons 'with smiles.' Smiles! Your husband then is—what! not your friend? Win him with a falsehood, and keep him

with a mask—live under his eye, and cheat
him? As well kiss and slay him!

What then? How should I meet him?
Silently, if I might; dutifully, if I could;
tearlessly, if possible; faithfully still.

But how was I to get calmness? How
strive for that quiet of heart, that lull of
the pulses, raging and rioting now under
the goad of that monster in woman's form,
and rising up against my lover—my husband—my guardian watcher—my friend?
How *be* that unmoved humanity, with the
show of which he should never be beguiled
if I could not attain to it?'

Was ever such a woman born as that?
Had she ever rested on the great heart of
a man? Had little children ever looked
up to her in reverence? Had she sucked
mother's milk? If so, was it a hyena's?
Was she human or devil?

The air seemed loaded with ill vapours.
There was no breathing where that woman
had stood. The pure breath of heaven,
the atmosphere of home, was poisoned by
her.

I must breathe elsewhere. But where
should I go? I might meet him. I would
not meet him yet. I must be able when

he came, to take his hand quietly, and look
into his eyes, and read them. No one
could read them as I could. When I looked
into their clear depths, the soul opened all
its chamber doors, and showed me what was
within—heaped-up jewels, truth, honour,
steadfastness, tender heart-warmness, remorse for the slightest ill-doing, thankful-
ness for love, devotion to God.

There was a small observatory at the
top of the house. There the breeze would
be flowing, if anywhere. Thither I would go.

It was a long weary way to mount, but
I thought I could do it if I took my time.
And I did take my time. I reached it, and
was glad.

I looked out over the low-pillared balustrade across the landscape, now misty with
the damps of evening. The woods lay fair
and waveless, with their close-set heads,
taking counsel of the closing day. Fair,
too, showed hillock and moorland beyond.
Hamlet and scattered farmstead, with their
blue wreathing smoke, nestled quietly in the
heart of the hollows, with hayricks about
them, like piled gold for the use of the
dwellers. Shrub and lawn, pasture and
avenue, orchard and coppice, all looked

their stillest and fairest; and, through all,
like a silver thread, flowed the Eden river.

A fair landscape is nothing without a
movement of life.   Slowly down by a
sheltered woody path came on two figures,
passing from the direction of the Glebe
Farm towards one of the wee-walks farthest from the Grange, but belonging to its
pleasure-grounds.

One figure was very easily recognised
by me; it was that of my husband.   The
other was, to all appearance, Kitty.

With regard to the last figure, a few moments served to show me my mistake.

As the two persons reached a secluded
nook, hid from all eyes but those which
were fixed in amazement on them from
the height of the observatory wall, the
second figure dismantled.   Kitty's bonnet
was thrown off by the hand of the wearer.
Not so was Kitty's old cloak that draped
and disguised the drooping form which I
beheld.   That was carefully unfastened at
the clasped throat, and thrown off by
another hand.   That hand was my husband's.

The figure that now presented itself I
recognised in a moment.   It was that of

Mrs. Campbell. The marvellous grace of
that figure there was no mistaking. The
hair seemed arranged to take the form I
had seen it take when I looked upon her
in that dark London house. True, they
were just so far off that I could not have
seen the blue snood, had it been there.
Perhaps it was not there. How should it
be there, seeing that it had fallen that very
morning into my husband's bosom, crossed
and gold-threaded by a torn lock of hair,
where it must have caught and been de-
tached from the head of the wearer by a
button of his waistcoat!

Watch her!

Only think of that!

She lifts her arms to heaven, and then
casts them about his neck.

That will do, Jessaline—that is enough.

My limbs had no power to bear me up
any longer. I sank down on the pitiless
ground, and, half-sitting, half-leaning, laid
my arm against a projection of the stone
balustrade, and bowed my head upon it.

'Oh, Jessaline, Jessaline!' I cried in my
misery—'blue-snooded Jessaline!'

'Are those fair boys yours, Jessaline?
and who is their father? Are you privy

to your husband's slaying, and have you
bribed that bad man Clement Favrel to
hush it up? Who else has bribed him?—
tell me that, brow-banded Jessaline!'

'Could you meet him—him, the man I
looked upon almost as a god—could you
meet him nowhere but here, Jessaline? If
he is lost—if he is caught in your toils, the
fault is yours, Jessaline—the fault is yours,
not his, for you have snared him anew. In
your young days of innocence I could pity
you. *He* has been pure and true since
those long-ago days. But *you*, where have
you been Jessaline? In what foul ways
have you wandered, and what paths have
you trodden since then? Answer me that,
Jessaline. Where did I find you, and
what was James Roupe to you? How came
you hither, and for what have you come?
Oh Jessaline—Jessaline—Jessaline!'

How long I lay in that trance of misery,
resting or rocking or writhing against the
cold stones, I know nothing.

The first thing that roused me was the
sense of a presence. I was no longer alone;
I knew that quite well. By some strange
sympathy I was always well aware when
Ralph was in the same room with me,

whether I saw him enter it or not—whether
I heard him, or whether a carpet muffled
his tread. I knew now that he was standing
not far off.

I raised my face, and looked.

At the door of the observatory by which
I had entered he stood—stood like a god—
like Mercury newly alighted on some great
hill-top. One forward foot of surprise
seemed to steady him; the other—both
wore spurs for wings—the other had scarcely
passed clear through the door. On the
handle of that door one hand still rested,
as if he feared to loose it lest the click of
the hasp should startle me, and I should
rise suddenly and spring over the balustrade.
Across the arm so extended to the door-
handle behind him hung a crimson shawl,
caught up in haste to wrap me with, when
the idea had struck him that he might find
me here, and have to carry me down through
the draughts of the long galleries. It hung
like a banner rolled to the ground, backing
him with gorgeous folds and glorious hues.
His other hand was clenched, and the bent
raised knuckle of the forefinger set against
his lips, as if to shut in a sigh, or cry
'Silence !' to the winds, lest they should

move and stir me from my safety till he dared leap to my side.

I saw his terror, and I held out to him the hand on which I was not leaning.

Quietly now he drew to my side, sank on one knee before me, and wrapped the shawl round my chilled limbs. Next he took me up carefully in his arms, bore me down through the galleries, and laid me on my bed.

Not a word had been spoken between us all this time.

'My love,' he said at last, 'you are troubled. What is it?'

'Nothing,' I said—'nothing, at least, that you can help.'

'That will not do, Grace—that will not do for me.'

'I have no more to say.'

'Yes you have, my love—you have a great deal more to say to me. You have to tell me what you were doing with that salt of sorrel this morning. You thought no one saw you, my love; but I saw you. You refused my help upstairs; but I saw mischief in your face. I followed you up. You shut your dressing-room door, but you forgot that the other door was wide open, that led into this sleeping-room of ours. Well, my love, I got into this room by its outer door. I had some difficulty to find anything tall enough to hide me. I rolled myself into one of the window-curtains, and from that post I watched you. Before the powder you were dreaming of mixing in that glass could have reached your lips, I should have dashed it to the ground. *You* would not have fallen there, bruising your poor dear tender little body, but for the unlucky accident of one of my spurs getting entangled in the curtain.'

' Oh ! '

' What! the little magpie note again?

' Now, come, love, I have been quite open with you—and you will pardon my rudeness, I know, in stealing upon your privacy in that free-and-easy manner; I shall be more respectful when you are well again, Grace. I have been quite open with you, my love, and I shall expect you to be the same with me. You have something on your mind: tell me what it is.'

' I cannot.'

' Indeed, but you can; and what is more, you must.'

' Must ! '

'Yes, must.'

'You cannot make me speak.'

'Can I not? I shall try. Come, my
love, have you forgotten that I am your
husband?'

'Ah!'

'I think you cannot refuse me anything
that I ask of you seriously. So, tell me,
what is this that is weighing upon your
little heart?'

'I cannot—I never, never will tell you!'

'Grace, do you know that you are for-
getting yourself? Do you not see that you
are breaking your vow?'

'No—no—no!'

'But I tell you that you are. You are
loosening all the cords that bind us one
to the other by this withholding of your
confidence from me. If our love is not
peace and safety, and shared thoughts and
mingled souls, why then I'll none of it, I
forswear and have done with it for ever.'

'I would speak, but I dare not.'

'Dare not! Have I taught you to fear
me?'

'I have been wrong, I have indulged
evil thoughts. Do not force me to lower
myself in your eyes.'

'Nonsense, child! You are ill; you do not know quite what you are doing. You had a long sorrow, then a long sickness. You are not answerable for your thoughts. Come, open your heart to me, my darling: where would you turn for comfort, if not to me, Grace?'

'I cannot—cannot tell you, while you speak to me in that way: it makes my heart sore. If you were harsh and unkind, perhaps I might—though I do not think I could. But your voice is so sweet to me, your words are so tender—what can I— what can I do! what can I say!'

'Come, come! Out with it at once, Grace. Let us have no more folly. Make a clean breast of it, and pretty quick, too; I am rather tired of this sort of thing Are you dumb still? Come, then, I *insist* upon your telling me. This is the first time I have needed to use my authority; but I *will* use it now. Come, out with your secret, this instant!'

'It is no secret—you know it all.'

'Know all what?'

'The blue snood.'

'What, out of the magpie's nest?'

'No; with the gold hair upon it—

caught by your button—torn from the head
that wore it.'

'What more?'

'Kitty's bonnet and cloak.'

'What, those in the magpie's nest too!'

'No, no—don't laugh, don't laugh!——'

'Well, I will not. But what more have
you found in the magpie's nest?'

'Jessaline!'

'Bless my heart! I had no idea that the
birds in our paradise here built nests of
that enormous size. But I suppose it's all
right. If you remember, you were very
much struck with the queer ornithology
displayed in that altar-carving of the church
of St. Gudule at Brussels, wondered how
on earth such specimens found their way
into Eden. You are quite satisfied that
nature is all right now, I suppose? Have
you anything more to confess, my love?'

'Are you trying to baffle me, Ralph?'

'Was that speech quite worthy of you,
Grace? Come, come; if my light heart
does not speak for me, why, I must try some
other means to put you at rest. Grace,
look into my eyes! Nay, come, look at me
well. Never fear; stare me out of coun-
tenance, if you can; you are quite welcome.

Now, what do you read there? Are you quite satisfied?'

'Quite.'

'Tell me honestly, then—do I look like a man fit only for Bedlam or the hottest corner in hell? Say so, if you think it; pray don't mince matters. Let me know candidly if you consider that I look like a man with a great crime locked in his breast; with a slain wife shut in the house of his fathers, with a she-serpent hidden in his garden bower; with a stain on his name, and with a blot on his escutcheon?'

'No—no—no!'

'Do you want any further assurance?'

'No—none—none!'

'If you do, you shall have it, Grace. You shall have any assurance in the world that I can give you of my loyalty to you. I will swear any oath you like.'

'I will hear none.'

'Not one word?'

'Not one. Ralph!'

'My own darling?'

'Ralph!'

'Why do you falter, love? What is it?'

'Ralph, you are an angel.'

'Booted and spurred!'

'You are, Ralph.'

'Now just see the vanity of woman! You are thinking, I suppose, of a certain text—"And the sons of heaven saw the daughters of earth that they were *fair*; and they took unto themselves wives——"'

'Ralph, I should have died if you had not spoken to me as you have done. Your nobleness and truth have saved my life— and my boy's.'

'Why, you unmitigated little prophetess! who told you it would be a boy?'

'I am sure it will, Ralph: I have so longed to give you an heir.'

For once I was a true prophetess.

That night was born an heir to Fairfield Grange.

CHAPTER VII.

MOTHERHOOD.

Child of my heart! my sweet, beloved first-born!
Thou dove who tidings bring'st of calmer hours!
Thou rainbow who dost shine when all the showers
Are past—or passing! Rose which hath no thorn,
No spot, no blemish—pure and unforlorn—
Untouched, untainted! Oh, my flower of flowers!
More welcome than to bees are summer bowers,
To stranded seamen life-assuring morn!
Welcome—a thousand welcomes! Care, who clings
Round all, seems loosing now its serpent-fold:
New hope springs upward; and the bright world seems
Cast back into a youth of endless springs!

BARRY CORNWALL.

TRUST the soul of motherhood for a cure!
Trust those baby lips for healing! If
the heart were broken into fragments, those
infant arms would gather them up. If
the spirit were half quenched and dead to
earth, that small winged messenger would
bring down the spark to kindle it anew.

Grace Harcourt, snowy maiden that was,

where has your coldness melted and gone
to? Mrs. Colonel Elphinstone, steady-eyed
matron, pray what has become of your
equanimity?

When first I heard that little wonderful
cry, the world spun round in a dance, like
a huge top with that atom of a thing for a
pivot! The longing eyes strained to get a
sight of the treasure of treasures; the lips
mumbled at it, the heart panted for it, the
soul clave to it. It was the sole created
thing in the universe: all beside was blank.
Oh, the enfolding of that fairy trifle! the
touch of those little formless feelers which
would one day be lips, growing beneath my
kiss! Oh the consciousness of the presence
of presences! of the dream become reality,
the fancied joy actual! The delightful
realising of a wonder to which the 'Arabian
Nights' are nonsense! These and a thousand feelings akin to them were filling up
the small space that ringed round two
human creatures, a little and a big—I put
the baby first!—and all the rest was chaos!

The singular and culpable impertinence
with which great creatures in boots and
spurs treat these very important, but small,
facts of life, is as wonderful as it is pro-

voking. You hear nothing from them but
the oddest exclamations: 'Where are its
eyes?—a little blind puppy!' or 'What am
I to do with this long-tailed titmouse?' or
'Does it do nothing but suck ?' or 'What
is it puckering up its mouth in that
ridiculous manner for?' or 'It blinks at
the sun like a young owl,' or, worst and
more shameful of all, ' Take it away, nurse
—a little usurper!'

How different it was with Frau Hengler!
Only to see how that woman devoured that
child!

Frau Hengler!—Oh, I have forgotten to
say that Frau Hengler had come to us.
Dear, dear, that child puts everything
else out of my head!

Yes, that was Ralph's surprise for me.
I had told him of that wicked Mrs. Burlington having come to me with an offer
of a nurse of her own choosing, somebody
possibly after her own pattern whom she
seemed so anxious to palm off upon me.
Hearing this, and knowing that I must
have some help, he had remembered my
liking for this forlorn and kind-hearted
soul, Frau Hengler, and had written for
her to come and settle herself amongst us.

I think I never had a more pleasant surprise in all my life.

To watch Frau Hengler over that child,
was the most delightful thing imaginable—
except nursing it oneself. Her particular
fashion of nursing it was to walk about the
room with it held high up, horizontally,
in her hands, not in her arms, with its face
laid against her cheek. She was never
tired of that parade, and the child liked it
clearly.

But of all ridiculous things, the most
ridiculous was to watch Ralph take hold of
that child. It was enough to make the
babe itself fling up its legs and crow with
laughter! *He* took it exactly in the opposite way to Frau Hengler, perpendicu-
larly, with a hand each side its waist, just
as loosely and with as little show of caring
what he held up in that undistinguished
manner, as if it had been the king of the nine-
pins—bless its little round ball of a head!
—which he has picked up off the floor!

Then Ralph did everything he possibly
could to spoil its temper—which was that
of a kicking angel! He would lift it up,
just in that position I have described, for
me to kiss it. But no sooner were my lips

pouting—ready to reach 'that bourn' from which no mother's mouth 'returns' if it possibly can help it, than the poor little thing was suddenly lowered, like a descending 'jack-in-the-box' when the lid is shut down, and all that my lips met was—empty air!

It really *was* a pretty baby! It was never cross—never. And then what a wonderful variety there was about it! Why, it was a perfect camelion for colour! First it was red, then it was yellow, and then it was white and waxen as the little pale stars of the evergreen holly. And it never took the same tints twice. When it emerged out of the white-waxy phase, it changed to the loveliest blush colour all over that ever was seen! And at that it staid.

What shall I say about its eyes? Of course they were deep blue; I had taken good care of that—I should think so! What is the good of having a pattern, if one does not know how to copy it? When those eyes were twinkling all over with fun and frolic which they knew nothing whatever about, but wished to make it appear that they did, then the corners of its mouth were exceeding like——What a

pity and a shame it is that we cannot be
content with a thing just for what it is
and nothing more, but must go puzzling
oneself about resemblances, and all that
sort of figurative nonsense: but so it is,
and so I suppose it will be to the end of
time—if there ever does come an end of
time in which there are no more babies.

And how did Ella take it? Poor Ella,
she had been sadly neglected lately. But
I think the new doll made amends for all.
It was beautiful to watch the instinctive
comfortableness with which she took it in
hand. When Ralph first took hold of it,
I could scarcely repress an infant scream.
I felt so sure he would drop it—he didn't,
though, I am happy to record. But when
it found its way into Ella's arms it seemed
to be naturalised there at once.

During the last half-year Ella had been
springing up in a most alarming manner.
She was now almost tall enough to reach
as high as Marian's shoulder, and that was
saying a good deal. Then she had lost a
great deal of her extreme childishness of
manner, remaining still, however, the simple
child she ever was in all else; the free,
frank English girl; the fairest rose of our

garden; the purest pearl that ever left ocean for land.

If anything were wanted to make the dawn of a gracious womanhood lovelier in Ella's face than it was before, it was that sweet and serious beauty that stole over it when she took my little Ralph into her arms. Perhaps that was only a mother's fancy; but then his father said so too.

Now Ella little knew, and certainly never dreamed, who she was folding in her arms, locking to her loving young heart, when she nursed that first baby of mine, and Ralph's. She thought she was fondling a little person of no particular consequence; but only his high and mightiness, Ralph Flemming Elphinstone, the fairy lord of the Elfin Stone, the heir of Fairfield Grange, the pride and joy of his father's heart, and the delight of his mother's eyes. He was all this, it is true, the little rogue! But he was something more than all this too. He was to be something very particular indeed to Ella. What could that be? Well, I do not know that it need be any very great secret. The fact was that when Ella was nursing that boy of ours, she was unconsciously nursing her future son-in-law!

.

CHAPTER VIII.

A COUNCIL OF TWO.

It has been a canker in
Thy heart from the beginning.

BYRON.

I HAVE now reached that point in my brief
and imperfect sketch of our own home lives
where all the clouds which had for awhile
dulled our happiness, were finally rolled
away. The peace of our days was safe for
the future. Here, then, were I writing for
other eyes than those of my children,
my narrative should perhaps, artistically
speaking, come to a close, as the fragment
of a life-history, assuming to be nothing
more. No explanations of the past, so far
as my husband was concerned, were desired
or needed by me to bring out that large
faith in his truth and goodness, and that
admiration of his noble nature, which had
grown up side by side with my love for

him. But though the honour of our house
seemed now fully assured, still all that
strange drama was not yet played out, the
masked actors in which had involved our
lives in troubles not of our own seeking,
and in mysteries hateful and mischievous
alike to us both. The root and spring of
all our fears and uncertainties it is fitting
that our children should know, in order
that blame, if blame should hereafter arise
touching any member of their father's
house, may fall upon the really blamable
and not upon the innocent; and that, if in
the future any blemish should seem to rest
upon a hitherto unsullied name, they—our
beloved children—at least may know where
the truth lies.

As I proceed, it will be said very probably that I have quitted the fair field of
legitimate narrative, and am writing not a
life-history but a melodrama. Against that
charge I have nothing to reply, except that
I am in reality not open to the censure
involved in it. Life is life; and I cannot,
consistently with a due regard for truth,
alter or amend its conditions and issues.
Stranger than fiction, more grotesque than
pantomime, as it often is, we are bound to

take it as we find it, or leave its records
altogether untouched.

In the events which follow, my husband
and I had, too, as will be seen, a most close
and intimate concern; and if those events
did not involve so painful a personal con-
flict as others hitherto recorded, they yet
brought with them full as strong, and
absorbing, and heart-warm an interest.
This will readily be understood when it is
shown how close was the tie between us
and those into whose fortunes we now
threw ourselves heart and soul—ay, with
one heart and one soul; for we two,
Ralph and I, had never more an unshared
interest or a divided thought.

I had now returned to my own old vigorous condition of body. I could take long
walks, be my husband's constant companion again; had no cares, for I had Frau
Hengler and Ella always about my boy,
when Ralph and I were not with him; and
I began now to look about me for the
duties my long ailing condition had obliged
me to forego. It had been a bitter pain to
me to put those duties from me, and I prepared to take them up now, joyfully.

'Ralph,' I said, 'I am quite able to assist

you now in that matter you more than once referred to. What is it, and what can I do to help you?'

'Are you quite sure that you are as well and as strong as I would have you, Grace?'

'Yes, quite, Ralph.'

'I am anxious on this head, my love, because, although you may not be subjected to fatigue of body, you will have to meet much that is likely to disturb your mind.'

'Never mind that: we will bear the burthen between us.'

'It is a long story, Grace. Come into the Hermitage, and let us have it out there.'

To the Hermitage we went; and there Ralph opened his budget.

'I must begin a good way back,' he said; 'for the beginning of the story I have to tell dates about five and thirty years since.

'In the year 1790 my father and mother were travelling in the Highlands of Scotland, partly for amusement and partly on a visit to my mother's relations there—she was a Douglas, you know. While there, my mother gave birth to a daughter, and

died. My father never looked up after-
ward. This is a common state of things
among the Elphinstones. They are as
constant as Mandarin ducks, Grace, that
never mate again. It will happen that the
Elphinstones do sometimes, but that is a
rare exception, and only occurs when—as
in my case—the wrong mate has been
chosen, and the affections have been
baulked.

'For a long time nothing could induce
my father to return to Fairfield. This
place had been the scene of all the happiness of his married life, and he could not
bring himself to face it without that dear
companion who had walked these paths as
you walk them with me, Grace. It was
years before he returned home from Scotland.

'Another painful part of the story was
that he could not bear the sight of the
child whose birth had cost him the life of
its mother. But for me the poor little
soul would have had no one to care for her,
till, strangely and touchingly enough, an
old grey-headed man fell in love with the
child.'

'Ralph, pardon my interrupting you,

my dear love; surely Jessaline is your sister?'

'Of course; who else could she be? Or rather you should say, Emmeline. You are thinking it strange, I dare say, that I can speak so calmly on this subject now; but you will see, when I come nearer the end of my story, what a complete revolution you have caused in some of my most rooted feelings, what a change your dealings with me have worked in the more morbid part of my nature. I owe you much, my wife!

'I have already told you so much of the old man's—Mr. Campbell's—story, love, in connection with my sister's early days, that I need not go into it again now. It is sufficient if I account to you for the somewhat odd accident of your never having heard that I had a sister living. The fact was, that old Mr. Campbell would not be happy unless he could be allowed to consider the child altogether in the light of his own daughter; and when my father at last resolved to return to his neglected estates, this eccentric old man took the unwarrantable course of putting advertisements into all the papers, announcing her death. She

should, he said, be entirely his own, and
no one should have a right to claim her
any more. My father, a little ashamed, I
suspect, of having disliked and neglected
the child, and then made her over to a
stranger, did not care to contradict the
report; but stipulated with Mr. Campbell
that he should follow him from Scotland to
Fairfield, live near the Grange, and should
never remove the child farther away. And
when my father returned home with me,
we being both still in the deepest mourning
for my mother, no questions were pressed
upon him; for everyone knew how morbid
and unreasoning his dislike had been to the
child, and how deep his grief still was for
that beloved wife whose loss had made the
poor little girl so intolerable in his sight,
from the hour of that wife's death.'

'What great command you must have
had over your feelings when so young, and
even over your speech, Ralph, to keep such
a secret—and such a needless secret—from
curious questioners.'

'I think it was not so much from any
natural aptitude for shutting myself up,
Grace, as from a sense of what was owing
to my father. No one knew what he had

suffered so well as I did, and at first I was careful not to tell tales, because I knew he would be made wretched to have the child talked about. Later, as I grew older, I felt the whole arrangement to be so singular and ill-advised, that I was really, then, so much ashamed of the long hoax that had been played off alike upon friends and neighbours, that my tongue was tied.

' I am now coming to the painful part of my story, and some of its details I must hasten over, for I cannot bear to think or to speak of them.

' At the time when the news of my poor little playfellow's elopement reached me, I had just got my commission, and had been ordered, with the rest of us, abroad. What means I could employ at a distance from home for her recovery, and if not that, for her support under whatever difficulty she might have to struggle with, I, of course, did employ. My father could do nothing; he was disabled by illness, and soon afterwards died.

' I may as well say here, what you will pretty well have guessed to be the case, knowing my peculiarities as you now know them. The disgrace of that elopement, and the possibility—nay, the likelihood—that things were worse than after all they turned out to be; the stain that would be cast in such a case on my father's house and honourable name; made me keep the secret rigidly on my own account, the moment I was the sole living creature to be affected by it. My father and old Mr. Campbell both died the same year. The secret became mine alone; and I have kept it till this day.'

'You need not have kept it from me, Ralph; I might have lightened your burthen by sharing it with you.'

'I could not endure to speak to you of so hateful a story.'

'I do not understand. I thought you said that young Mr. Campbell married her.'

'He did. I ascertained that fact—no matter how, it is unimportant—beyond a doubt. But, before you became my wife, I had been shocked and wrung to the soul by intelligence that reached me of a second elopement. Grace, you remember that illness I had, when I told you that an old wound of mine had broken out afresh?'

'Perfectly. We could not think why

you suffered from such a miserable depression of spirits.'

'Truly it was an old wound, for I had suffered the same pain when I had feared at first that my sister had been betrayed by young Campbell; but this second breaking out of the sore that was healed over, was a worse pang than the first blow had caused me. Grace, I can tell you anything now, and you have deserved my fullest, freest confidence; yet, my beloved wife, I can hardly bring myself to utter the words. Grace, my wretched sister left her husband's roof. You know where I found her.'

'Oh, Ralph!'

'That she had voluntarily withdrawn herself from her husband's house in favour of some more questionable retreat was the news that had reached me when you saw me thrown on a sick bed. But when I recovered, I began to doubt the fact. It seemed to me so monstrous, so utterly impossible a thing for a sister of mine to do, that I could not bring myself on mature deliberation to believe it. My only informant was an agent I had employed in London for years to remit certain sums of money to my sister occasionally, as she might have need of them. That man was James Roupe.'

' James Roupe! ' I cried.

' Ay! only think of my employing that scoundrel! He professed to have known of her flight from her husband's house some years before he told me of it; but had kept the knowledge from me in the hope of being able to trace her retreat without my being put to the pain of knowing the fact. I employed him to pursue the enquiry by every possible means—without, however, of course, confiding to him my relationship to Emmeline. But no clue could he ever obtain—so he said—to her retreat.

' The very first hint I obtained—and that brought me at once the miserable conviction both of her fault and how I had been duped by Roupe—the first clue was that letter in the handwriting of my sister, addressed to the man Roupe, here at Fairfield, and which was sent on to our house from Mr. Sheringham's; that letter which, missing him (you had dismissed him already for his impertinence to you, you remember), fell into my hands to be redirected.'

' That was, then, why you went to the

bureau to compare the handwriting on that letter, when you found all in such disorder there?'

'It was. My sister had formerly written to me herself to assure me of her marriage, confirming by her own testimony the evidence I had already procured of the marriage having taken place in Scotland. I compared the writing, and jumped at once to the true conclusion, that my sister was to be found actually in Roupe's own house.'

'And you undertook that journey to London to——'

'To be assured one way or the other. And now, Grace, before I proceed with my miserable story, let me once and for all say just one word in extenuation of my frightful brutality to you—visiting the sins of the guilty upon your innocent head!'

'That has all been forgotten long ago, Ralph.'

'Grace, if ever a man builds upon the entire purity of any human creature, that one is his sister. All that is sacred and hallowed from every evil thought hovers round that angel minister to his boyhood's pleasures. A young man cannot conceive f any evil touching her, so sacred she seems
o

in his eyes.   If she falls, a star has dropped
from the heavens.   Her lapse from right
makes all other iniquity in the world possible. If she is sullied, who shall be pure?'

' Ralph, I saw quite well the state of mind
you were in when you came straight from
that wretched house to me.   Say no more
about it—tell me of Emmeline.'

' My sister emphatically denied that she
was living in Roupe's house.   But I would
not hear her.'

' Ralph, your sister is blameless—I will
stake my life on it!   Is she at the Glebe
Farm now?'

' She is.'

' I will go to her, Ralph.'

' You will do no such thing, my dear.
I am not going to subject you to any such
contact, I can tell you.'

' Ralph, you are very wrong.   What harm
can she possibly do to me in any case? Besides it is my duty, love.   When I married
you I married all that belonged to you.   I
claim my right in all that you possess.
Your sister is not your sister only, she is
mine as well.   I am quite determined to
go to her, Ralph.'

' Well, well, we will discuss that question

another time. Hear me out. I have work for you to do; but it is not that. I have had several long conversations with Emmeline since I went up to London to fetch her down to the Glebe; and I must give you in as few words as I can the heads of the story she told me.

'The marriage between her and young Campbell was entirely a love-match. They lived very happily together till these twins were born——'

'Walter and Heine?'

'Yes, Walter and Heine; Walter you saw at once resembled me: many youths are far more like their uncles than their fathers. Heine, I conclude, is like his father, Neil Campbell, wherever that father may be.'

'Is he not dead?'

'It is to be feared he is; and by foul play. But let me get on with my story.

'Soon after the birth of the twins, something led Campbell to suspect that Emmeline was an Elphinstone, and not, as the old man his father had told him, the child of poor Scotch parents whom his father had brought from the Highlands and adopted. She refused to answer certain questions he put to her on the subject, for two reasons.

In the first place, because it would pain me
to have the story known—which story moreover, I believe, she had pledged herself to
old Campbell never to reveal; and, in the
second place, because Campbell was, she
soon found, a needy spendthrift, who had
married her to secure the fortune his father
had destined for her, and who now, being
foiled in that (for the old man's money was
nowhere forthcoming) was anxious to prey
upon any relations of hers who might prove
to be well off. To force her into compliance,
he threatened to take the children from
her. There she at once broke down. She
kept her secret still ; but the scoundrel
broke her heart. She lived in one perpetual
agony. Every time the brute was short of
money, he would take the children and hide
himself away with them. Then he would
write to her, urging her to a confession of
the truth; and swearing that if she did not
either tell him who she belonged to, or use
her influence to obtain funds from her relations to throw away upon bubble com-
panies and bubble schemes, he would take
the boys out to Canada, ·and she should
never see them again. During one of these
attacks upon her goaded mother-heart, she

determined to go to James Roupe, the agent through whom, as I told you, I had repeatedly forwarded money to her. Her intention was to ask him to advance her a present sum, sufficient to bribe her tyrant to give her back her boys; and if that did not have the desired effect, she had resolved in her own mind to throw herself upon me for further assistance. Oh, that she had! Oh, that she had done so before going to that man's house!'

'Could she get no redress? Had Campbell a right to rob her of her children without any fault on her part?'

'Unfortunately he had, Grace. A woman is but a chattel in the eyes of the law. Her children are no more hers than they are the Pope's, if you come to litigate the matter. The woman brings a soul into the house, and the man brings a cudgel. And when her children are born to her, and she has so many more fine nerves through which to be feelingly alive to the knife that cuts deepest, he can take her in hand at his will, and serve her as your cook would serve your lampreys, if you would let her—tear off those fine woven tissues that cling and palpitate about her, and cast her down to earth

bare, bleeding, writhing in agony—worse,
worse than dead!'

'Oh, Ralph.'

'That was my sister's cross—and a fiery
cross it was. Then came her fall. How
that happened is a mystery to me. She
had sought Roupe as I tell you, and he
offered to set the law to work to get back
her children. At this point her narrative
broke down. She could, I dare say, have
spoken of what followed rather to anyone .
than to me.'

'She would tell me?'

'Perhaps. Meanwhile it is past help.
Roupe is dead—beyond the reach of my
vengeance—another victim to the bursting
of those bubble schemes which have brought
so many men to ruin during this past year
of 1825.'

'And what became of Neil Campbell?'

'He did go abroad. He took the children,
as he had threatened, to Canada. There,
he was most likely murdered. The boys
returned to England when grown up, in
the company of Clement Favrel, bearing
his name.'

'Lady Letty seemed to me to think

Clement Favrel must have murdered Neil
Campbell.'

' I fear so. He must have pumped him
well first, too. He seems to have got from
him the possible whereabouts of Old Campbell's money-bags by the constant digging
he is engaged in——'

' Oh, Ralph, how unfortunate! Here are
Walter and Ella coming, and your story
not finished.'

' Never mind; I will finish it another
time.'

CHAPTER IX.

STUBBORN YOUTH.

Thou divine nature, how thyself thou blazon'st
In these two princely boys ! They are as gentle
As zephyrs, blowing below the violet,
Not wagging his sweet head : and yet as rough,
Their royal blood enchafed, as the rudest wind
That by the top doth take the mountain pine,
And make him stoop to the vale. 'Tis wonderful,
That an invisible instinct should frame them
To royalty unlearn'd ; honour untaught ;
Civility not seen from other ; valour
That wildly grows in them, but yields a crop
As if it had been sow'd.   *Cymbeline.*

WE were not long interrupted.   Ella Stuart
and Walter Favrel—as we shall still call
him—hailed us, spoke a few words of greeting, and then passed on their way, bright
and buoyant in youth and beauty.   They
were far too much absorbed to take much
heed of us.

As soon as the two were out of ear-shot,
Ralph turned to me.

'Grace, do you mark those two ? I fear they are making a fatal mistake—a mistake sad for both, and terrible to one.'

'I almost fear so too, Ralph.'

'I would have given my right arm those two had never met. He loves that girl, if I am not much mistaken; yet she has no thought but for Robert Flemming. He loves her for her innocent blooming self; but she likes him only because he talks to her of her heart's idol.'

'The responsibility is a heavy one for you, Ralph—Walter being your nephew, too. Should you not let Captain Flemming know?'

'I wrote to him to that effect two days ago; his ship is in port now. But where was I in my story when these two winged creatures lighted down upon us?'

'You were telling me of Clement Favrel's having brought the young Campbells home from Canada.'

'Hang the mountebank! Let us talk no more of him. Yet, stay. You see what his game has been, do you not, with his pistol-shots and his eavesdropping behind haycocks?'

'Not exactly.'

'Why, he must have learnt from Neil
that there was every reason to believe Emmeline was an Elphinstone. The Elphinstone notions of family honour are pretty
notorious. To keep the secret of a sister's disgrace from getting wind, he would
be sure I should open my purse-strings to
a considerable extent. He has taken the
relationship between Emmeline and me
for granted, and has played his game accord-
ingly. As we did not call at the Glebe
House, he introduced himself in that singular manner. Had I shown any intention of appearing publicly against him for
a misdemeanor when he fired that shot
into my panel behind the shoulders of
Heine, he would have bought himself off
with a threat of making public Emmeline's
disgrace. In that exploit he was simply
feeling his way. So, too, with his eavesdropping that evening behind the haycock.
Since my return from Brussels the man has
made me his prey.'

'It was surely an ill-advised step, Ralph,
to give him that cheque he sent me to you
for.'

'You are right, as usual, Grace. I felt
I was a fool the moment I had done it. But

I had just welcomed those two gallant boys.
You were surprised at my reception of
them, Grace?'

'I was.'

'I dreaded lest the fellow, failing in his
attempt to victimise me, should make their
mother's disgrace public. There was nothing in the world, save his own interest,
to prevent his spreading abroad the report
that Emmeline was the runaway daughter
of the house of Elphinstone, the mistress of
a coarse London lawyer, and the mother of
Campbell's children—these so-called Favrel
brothers.'

'How did you learn they were Emmeline's children?'

'From Emmeline herself. I had taken
care she should not lose sight of me after
I had met her at Roupe's house. She wrote
to me at Brussels to tell me of Roupe's
suicide, which I had already seen noticed
in the paper. Just at the last, before he
destroyed himself, ruined in means and
ruined in character, he wrote her, it seems,
a farewell letter, which spoke more in his
favour than any other act of his life. In
it he told her that her children were in
England under a false name, and that they

were living at the Glebe House, as Mr.
Favrel's sons.'

'That was strange.   He did not seem to
know Heine.'

'I believe Roupe got his information
later during his visit to me.   He made,
it seems, good use of his time while at
the Grange, and hunted them up, lawyer
fashion.   How Heine came to recognise him
was from his pretended father, Clement
Favrel, having pointed Roupe out to him
one day in Fairfield village as the man who
had led his mother to desert her home.
Heine told me this.   When the two met
afterwards in our drawing-room, Roupe
not having then got his information about
them, of course he did not recognise the boy
Heine Campbell in the young man Favrel.

'But let us return to Emmeline.

'The one passionate desire of her heart
was now to see her boys; but the shrinking
dread of what might be her reception at
their hands held her back from seeking
them.   I wrote to her repeatedly, and at
last induced her to fall in with a scheme I
had hit upon to gratify this craving of her
heart.   You remember Kitty's random

shot—her suggestion of what a fine post of observation the "birdcage" room afforded to anyone desiring to see into the enemy's camp, the Glebe House?'

'I remember.'

'That suggestion I adopted. I brought Emmeline Campbell to the farm, and gave Kitty directions to attend to her, without raising a suspicion that anyone inhabited that portion of the building; and from her retreat behind the curtain of that "birdcage window"—the very window from which she eloped with Niel — Emmeline daily feasts her eyes upon the faces of her children.'

'Ralph, I have said before that you are an angel; I repeat my words now.'

'A man is but a blunderer in things celestial, my dear wife. It is your ministry that I want now: you are nearer the Eternal than I, Grace.'

'Tell me what I can do for Emmeline.'

'This: bring her children to her arms, if it be in human power to move them. They loathe her very name. That is her present cross.'

'Have you spoken to them?'

'I have sounded them both, and they are both as stubborn as the very deuce. I can make nothing of them.'

'Do they know their mother is here, or that she is your sister?'

'Of course not. They would fly to the other end of the earth if they thought they should meet her here.'

'How shall I attack them?'

'Your own way: be guided by your own instincts. You are a mother now, and know the strength that lies in the clasp of those infant fingers.'

'I have more hope of Walter than I have of Heine: Heine is a little stubborn; Walter is frank and generous.'

'Both natures are fine. Heine is firmer than Walter, and, once won, will be the more stable, perhaps, of the two. Their very persistency in refusing to see their mother shows how right-minded they are; their hatred of her is but an offshoot of their feeling of repugnance for what is evil. They loathe the sin in her, and her for the sin.'

My husband ceased speaking. I was pondering over the difficulty of the task before me, and he was somewhat lost in thought, when we heard a sound of hurried footsteps.

The next moment Ella came rushing at full speed into the summer-house, and threw herself into my arms in a passion of tears.

'Oh, Mrs. Elphinstone! what shall I do—what shall——'

'Ella!' cried my husband in his surprise, starting up instinctively to seek Walter.

I laid my hand on his arm to stop him.

'Ella,' I said, 'what is the matter?'

'Oh, I shall never forgive myself! Walter says he loves me. He says I led him to believe that I loved him. He is so unhappy. He is coming to ask Colonel Elphinstone for me. But I told him—indeed I told him it was of no use. I cannot listen to him; I will not hear him; you know, you know I love Robert!'

'Did you tell him so, Ella?' questioned my husband.

'Oh no! I could not tell him that; but you know I never loved anyone but Robert—I cannot love anyone but Robert.'

'Calm yourself, my sweet Ella,' I said. 'Leave Colonel Elphinstone to speak to Walter.'

But before I could take her into the
house, for which purpose I rose to leave
the Hermitage, Walter was upon us.

'Walter,' said my husband, 'you have
forgotten yourself strangely to startle this
poor child as you have done.'

'Pardon me, my Ella!—pardon me,
Colonel Elphinstone! I had no intention—
I—I love her. I meant to ask you for
her—I had no intention of speaking to her
without your permission; but my love was
too strong for me—my heart overcame me.
Oh, my Ella! forgive me. I would die to
save you one moment's pain. Mrs. Elphinstone, speak for me—pray speak for me!'

'Give me your arm, Walter,' I said.
'Ralph, take Ella home.'

But the youth looked wistfully at Ella.

'Ella,' I said, 'you must forgive him,
child. And give him your hand a moment, or
he will not be happy: if you must lose him
as a lover you need not lose him as a friend.'

Poor Ella hung down her head, but gave
him her hand as she was bidden. The youth
took it in both his own, thanking her only
with his eyes.

As soon as Ralph had taken her away, I
took a turn up and down with Walter. His

heart was much softened just then, and I
thought that, if I could once turn his
thoughts away from Ella—no easy matter
at such a moment—I might feel my way
a little on the subject of his mother.

'You will speak for me, Mrs. Elphinstone?' he said.

'I will do all that can be done,' I answered; 'but you really must not speak to
Ella any more in this way. Put this affair
into my husband's hands. You are very
young. You cannot have a better guide
than he. Treat him as if he were your
father—trust him.'

'Do you think he will plead my cause?
do you think Ella will listen to him?'

'Am I to speak quite honestly to you?'

'Pray do.'

'I do not feel quite sure that he will
plead your cause with Ella.'

'Why? what have I done?'

'You have been a little premature, Walter—a little too hasty. Ella is almost a
child. My husband, I think, will not urge
a suitor upon her for some years to come,
even if she remains under our care. But
Captain Flemming is her guardian, not
Colonel Elphinstone.'

' Then I will appeal to Captain Flemming.   There is no trial he can put me to
that I will not undergo to win Ella.'

' Be patient, then, and wait till Captain
Flemming comes.'

' When will he come?   Is he likely to
be soon at Fairfield?   Can I find him?
Shall I go to him?'

' Now, do try to be patient.   I think it
likely that we may see him before very
long.   Meanwhile, I do not think I must
ask you to come up to the house till I know
what the Colonel thinks about it.   Will
you meet me in the Hermitage at this hour
to-morrow?'

' Gladly, thankfully.   Dear Mrs. Elphinstone, how can I be grateful enough to
you!'

' Nay,' I said, rather conscious that I had
another purpose in meeting him there
than that of forwarding his love-suit—
' nay,' I said, ' do not misunderstand me; I
cannot say one word to Ella on this subject.
All I can do is to come to you to-morrow,
and tell you what my husband says.'

' You are very kind.   God bless you,
Mrs. Elphinstone.   I wish I had any means
of showing my sense of your kindness.'

'I will remind you of that speech, Walter, when I want your good offices.'

'I hope you will—pray do.'

'And now you will do your best, I know, to be tractable and patient.'

'That is out of the question; I cannot promise that.'

'Well, well—I suppose you will be anxious. And now, good-bye, my dear young friend. This time to-morrow, remember. Be sure I shall not fail you.'

'Good-bye, dear Mrs. Elphinstone, and God for ever bless you!'

I was about to quit him and return to the house; but he still held the hand I had stretched out to him in farewell. He seemed as if he could not tear himself away from one who could speak to him of Ella: that was just how Ella had held him, as it were, by the button, to hear him talk about her beloved Robert.

'Oh, Mrs. Elphinstone!' he cried, 'what is to become of me if I fail to win her?'

'Do you think you could reconcile yourself to her loss,' I said, 'if it were to turn out that she would be happier with some one else?'

'I cannot lose her—I will not give her

up. Good God! Mrs. Elphinstone, you do
not mean to tell me that she loves another?'

'I do not mean to tell you anything of
the kind ; but I should like to see you
consider her happiness before your own.'

'It is not in human nature to forget
self so utterly—not now, at least, not now
—the wound is so deep—the pain is so
new.'

'No, I suppose it is not possible. There
is no love but one which can stand that
crucial test of self-renunciation. A mother's
heart alone is capable of sacrificing self for
what it loves. That is the sole, limitless,
imperishable bond in nature. Mothers
have been known—nay, I know one myself—mothers have been known to be entrapped even into a show of guilt through
their devotion to their children. Yet what
is the issue? Their children grow up—
sons, perhaps, like you, Walter—men who
know love only in its selfishness—and she
is despised and trodden under foot by those
who should at least remember that it was
in their cause she incurred blame.'

'Mrs. Elphinstone, what do you mean?'

'Shall I tell you, Walter? You see
quite well I am not generalising in what I

have said. I know your history. You have a mother——'

'I will not speak of her, Mrs. Elphinstone. Let me go!'

But I held him now as he had held me.

'Do you suppose for one moment,' I said, 'that, if all other things were in your favour, we could think of bestowing our Ella on a man who is an unnatural son to the most miserable and most devoted mother that ever lived — nay, the most ill-used? for, in spite of all appearances, *I* still believe——'

'Unhand me, Mrs. Elphinstone!'

'A son,' I went on without heeding him, 'a son who, without question, takes a bad man's word against his own ill-used, injured mother—a villain's verdict against a wronged and tortured woman!'

'Nothing—nothing on this earth can make excusable a wife's untruth. I really am astounded, Mrs. Elphinstone, that you, *you* of all people in the whole world, should treat such a lapse from purity and honour so lightly.'

'I forgive you the impertinence of that speech,' I said; 'you seem to forget that I

assert my belief in your mother's innocence.
But what I cannot forgive you for is your
passionate hatred of your mother. I know
what motherhood is now; and if I thought
a child of mine could ever indulge against
me such a wicked and unchristian spirit of
hatred as you are showing at this moment,
I should curse the hour it was born.'

I took his other hand, held him fast by
both, and looked straight into his eyes.

'What right have you,' I asked, 'to
judge your mother? what do you know of
her? Have you ever sought her? Have
you ever even taken the trouble to enquire
what has become of her? Suppose I know
more about her than you do? Suppose
I can show you, as I think I can, that,
seeking her children, she was entrapped;
that to recover you—you and Heine—
to save you from the example of a worthless father—she appealed to a villain for
help, and in her weakness and her sorrow,
with none beside to help her, forgot appearances, forgot the world—and all for you.
How is it you never thought of visiting
this sin upon your father's head? Who
was it that wrung her soul to madness?
Your father. Who was it that made her

mother's love a curse to her, instead of the blessing God meant it to be? Your father. Have you never thought of blaming him as the cause of all this evil? God will judge differently from man, Walter Favrel. I will tell you plainly, I would not trust a man with the keeping of a girl's peace who has so little true manhood about him as you have shown in this.'

'You are very hard — very unfeeling, Mrs. Elphinstone!'

'Walter Favrel, I am a mother.'

'What is it you ask of me?'

'Only this—a patient hearing. If I can show you that your mother has been belied, that her error is not of quite so deep a die as it has been made to appear to you, will you strive to crush out this rancour from your heart, this hateful hate towards the breast that nursed and cherished you?'

'She has disgraced the name we bear; that can never be made white again. She has made it a shame to us, and we have renounced it.'

'I repeat, I do not believe it. Your father disgraced nature in his wrongs against her motherhood. Was that no crime? Oh shame, shame on you men! You call us weak;

yet you expect from us a strength of which you are not capable yourselves. You turn our blood to gall, and then expect it to flow like water. You give us your selfish liking, and we barter for it a self-renouncing love. You rob us of our children, and bid us be calm and cool and cautious, and wear in our bosoms a stone in place of a heart.'

'What am I to do?'

'I have told you your duty—do it.'

'I will not see her.'

'I do not ask it. Walter Favrel, I am far from wishing to see you less sensitive on points of honour. But will you do what I ask of you? Will you simply try to shut out all past convictions, all thoughts that condemn your mother until you know more about her? That is all I desire just yet—all I ask till we meet again.'

'I will,' he answered.

And so I left him.

CHAPTER X.

A SCOUNDREL'S DEVICE.

I prayed aloud,
In anguish and in agony—
Upstarting from the feverish crowd
Of shapes and thoughts that tortured me!
Sense of intolerable wrong!
And whom I scorned, those only strong!
COLERIDGE.

THE next morning, when breakfast was over, after I had laid my boy in the arms of Frau Hengler, either to close up his little flower-buds of eyes in sleep, or to wake up and suck those pearl-beads of knuckles of his, I dressed myself for going out of doors, swept downstairs as light as a feather, and sought my Ralph in his study.

'Ralph,' I said, 'I want the key of the Glebe.'

'I have mislaid it in my pocket, Grace.'

'Then turn your pocket inside out, and

look for it. I must have that key of the Glebe, Ralph.'

'Grace, that key is not going to leave my pocket.'

'Ralph, that key is going to find its way into mine—unless, indeed, you choose to walk with me.'

'What makes you so urgent to have it just now?'

'I had a long talk with Walter yesterday.'

'Then why in heaven's name didn't you say so before?'

'Why, all yesterday we were taken up with Ella, and with visitors, or one thing or other. Come, give me the key.'

'What did Walter say?'

'If you are not busy—if you can walk with me part of the way to the Glebe, I will tell you as we go, Ralph. My dear husband, I do believe I shall win the day. But indeed, love, to do any real good I must see Emmeline at once—now, this very day, before I meet Walter again, as I have promised, in the Hermitage at three o'clock. I believe in Emmeline's innocence; but I must have her story from her own lips.'

Ralph rose, took his hat, and we went out together.

'Now, Grace, let me hear what you have done,' he said. 'But, first—here, just take charge of this key of the Glebe, will you? You had better have it at once; there will be no grace in my giving it to you when you have reasoned me out of it. I give up the point. I will take your word for it, love, that it is the best thing that can be done.'

'Thank you, Ralph; that is like you; you could not be a tyrant if you tried.'

'I am not going to try—at present.'

I then told him all that had passed between Walter and me.

By the time I had ended my story, we found ourselves close to the Glebe walls. Ralph took me round to the back entrance, promised to call for me at twelve o'clock, and, having turned the key for me, for the lock was rather stiff, left me to announce myself.

I wondered that he did not go in with me, and I told him so. His answer was that he could not endure to see me kiss her, and he felt sure I should; so did I.

All was very hushed as I entered the

'bird-cage' room. At first I thought
there was no one there. But on looking
at the window more narrowly, I there dis-
cerned a figure—it was Emmeline's. Her
dress was of the same colour as the curtain
of the window—a deep mazarine blue—and,
like the draperies of the window, watered.
In short, the dress corresponded exactly
with the curtains, except in texture, and
was doubtless chosen with a view to the
concealment of the wearer when she should
take up her post of observation where she
now stood. Her face was hidden from my
view; for one cheek was pressed to the
wall close to the edge of the window, and
the other was shaded by the curtain, as
her head was inserted between that curtain and the wall. The eyes that looked
out so intently must have had their sense
so quickened as to deaden all other senses,
for I spoke in vain.

'Sister.'

Still no answer.

'Sister.'

Not a movement yet.

'Sister.'

I began now to fear that, if she were to
look round, so entirely preoccupied as she

was, my presence would startle her dreadfully, perhaps even produce a fit.

My surprise was at its height when she turned slowly round and faced me, with a wan smile on her sweet face.

'I knew you would come,' she said; 'I heard you were there; but Walter was still at the window, and I could not move till he turned away. I am greedy of his face, sister; I have not seen it so long.'

We put our arms round each other, and it seemed that there was nothing to explain. Looking at her face now when its expression was less troubled than it had been when I had met her last in the dark London house—now when it was suffused all over with an innocent and divine tenderness—I saw at once what had been the charm of that face to me, which made me kiss her instinctively. She was the image of her brother; I saw my Ralph in every sweet line of her face.

Walter, then, was like his mother, of course; and in her face, too, I now saw a less marked likeness to Heine. Heine probably, I thought, and as my husband had suggested, resembled more fully his dead— perhaps murdered—father.

We two, Emmeline and I, sat down on the sofa to converse as if we had known each other all our lives. I found no difficulty in drawing from her all her story, which I need not repeat, since it has already been told in my husband's words—all her story, I should say, up to a certain point. There she broke down, exactly as she had broken down in speaking on the subject to her brother.

Seeing that the time was slipping by, and that I was no nearer to the object of my coming, I begged her to forget that we had so newly met, to remember that I was her sister, and to confide in me fully and freely. I told her that I had already made some impression upon Walter, that I had spoken of her in perfect faith, that she was more to be pitied than condemned; and called upon her earnestly, implored her by her love for her children, to justify me in what I had said by a full relation of the whole particulars of her withdrawal from her husband's house.

'There is really very little to tell,' she said, 'beyond what my brother already knows; but that little it was impossible to enter upon to him, prejudiced as he

already was against me by the account
Mr. Roupe had given to him years ago
of my flight from my husband's house, as
well as by that unfortunate accident of his
encountering me in London in the very
house of that man.'

Here Emmeline paused.

'It was that day,' she said at length,
'when I was driven almost to madness by
Campbell's taking my children away from
me, I sought Mr. Roupe, to ask him to
advance me some money which Campbell
had urged me to procure for him; for I
thought that, if I could get what Campbell
wanted, he would perhaps relent, and re-
store the children to me. I did not ask
any favour at Mr. Roupe's hands. I told
him that Colonel Elphinstone would make
good to him whatever he advanced to me
the moment he was applied to. I did not
go to Mr. Roupe's house, as I had generally done for remittances from my brother,
because Campbell had become very watchful of me, and was trying to find out my
secret—the secret of my being an Elphinstone, the sister of a rich and generous
brother, to whom I was indebted for a pro-
vision for my boys. But I wrote a note to

Mr. Roupe, begging him to send the money
to me by a trusty clerk, to an hotel, where
I should await his coming.

'Mr. Roupe came himself, but without
the money. He had, he said, sent his
clerk to procure cash in place of a cheque,
which he thought would be more convenient
to me.

'He sat down and conversed with me,
speaking, I thought, with great feeling and
kindness about my children. He knew, I
found, though I was careful not to betray
my husband's harsh dealing about the boys,
that Campbell had threatened to remove
them from me. He must have got that
knowledge, I suppose, from a servant, who
told me that she had met a strange gentleman, who had asked her some questions
about Mr. Campbell, whom he did not know.
Mr. Roupe said he wished I would put the
case into his hands, as he should like to try
what the law would do for me. But I told
him at once that I could not think of taking any legal steps against my husband; I
would rather trust that Campbell would
not carry out his intention of depriving me
of my children.

'While this talk was going forward upon

a subject so trying to me, and doubly painful from the fact that I was all the time
acting a part in striving hard to hide the
dread that was gnawing at my heart lest
I should lose my boys, the time was passing
on; and still the clerk never came.

'Mr. Roupe now changed the conversation. I began to see that he was himself
very curious to know in what connection
or relationship I stood to this Colonel
Elphinstone, from whom so much money
reached me through his—Mr. Roupe's—
hands. I had never, of course, told Mr.
Roupe that Ralph was my brother, nor
had my brother himself ever made that
fact known to his agent, Mr. Roupe. I
had nearly been surprised out of my secret,
however; for, after having conversed with
me for some time on indifferent topics, Mr.
Roupe suddenly made a most important
communication.

'"I came to speak to you myself, Mrs.
Campbell," he said, " because I wished you
to know at once that your sons are provided
for, for life. Colonel Elphinstone has employed me to draw up certain deeds of con-
veyance which will have the effect of adding
a still larger sum to the fortune already

placed at the disposal of each of your boys."

'Some expression of gratitude to my brother—always so good and generous—was on the point of bursting from my lips, when I was struck by a peculiarly watchful expression in Mr. Roupe's eyes, and at once checked myself. I had no idea what was passing through his mind then, but I had bitter cause to suspect it later.

'Some time longer was passed in detailing the particulars of the arrangement by which my boys were to be benefited; and still the clerk never came.

'I began now to feel seriously uneasy lest I should not receive the money that Campbell wanted in time to prevent his taking any final steps towards sailing for Canada, as he had threatened he would do.

'Seeing me troubled at the non-appearance of his clerk, Mr. Roupe at once offered to go back to his office, and return to me with the money himself.

'He did go; and he remained away for an unaccountable length of time—so long that it was getting quite dark night.

'When Mr. Roupe returned to the hotel where I was waiting, this was his story:

He had met Campbell, he said, seeking me. Campbell had returned home, leaving the boys at the wharf whence the vessel for Canada would sail, to ascertain if I had taken any steps to get him out of his difficulties. When he had reached home he had found that one of his creditors had put an execution into the house. Thereupon he had left the house again, setting out in search of me to prevent my returning home, since the bailiffs were in possession. Mr. Roupe had offered to convey Neil's message to me, which was to the effect that he wished me to remain at the hotel where I was, and that he would come to me there, after he had gone down to the docks to fetch away the boys. Mr. Roupe had told him that I was making arrangements to assist him out of his difficulties, and had left him in perfect good humour with me and the whole world. That was Mr. Roupe's story. It did not strike me at the moment to ask him how he had recognised my husband, whom I was not aware that he had ever seen, though I believe that my husband knew Mr. Roupe by sight.

'Mr. Roupe now rose to go. Before doing so, however, seeing me very jaded and

weary, he rang for the waiter to bring in
wine and biscuits. I thought him very
kind and feeling in his manner. I had
passed many an anxious and sleepless hour
before that fatal night, and I was by this
time quite worn out in strength and spirits.
I did not, therefore, refuse the glass of wine
he so kindly pressed upon me. I took it,
and for a moment felt revived.

'But I soon grew weary again. Seeing
this, Mr. Roupe bade me good night. I
gave him my hand very cordially, for he
had been more like a friend to me in his
manner than a mere man of business. Then
he left me.

'As soon as he was gone, it occurred to
me that he had forgotten after all to leave
with me the money for which I had waited
so long, and which I concluded he had
brought with him. But no matter, I
thought. It was all right now about Neil
and my boys, and I could seek Mr. Roupe
at his office in the morning—if, indeed, he
did not find out his mistake and despatch
the money to me in the meanwhile.

'Hour after hour I sat up, waiting and
hoping, but still Campbell did not come,
nor the boys.

' I began to have a thousand vague fears,
I thought at first something must have
happened to my children down at the docks,
where I knew that Campbell was very care-
less about them, leaving them to wander
about by themselves. Then I fancied that
he might have changed his mind, and taken
the voyage to Canada after all. I paced
up and down the room; I looked out of the
window, hoping yet to see them coming,
till I was almost blinded by the glitter of
the lamps, and the continual hurrying to
and fro of footsteps, which were not the
beloved footsteps that I longed to hear. I
could rest nowhere.

' At length the street grew silent. The
hotel doors were closed for the night, and
hopeless, tired, and sick at heart, I sought
the sleeping-room I had selected, looking
first sorrowfully round the little chamber
adjoining where I had thought to look upon
the sleeping faces of my children, and to
hear from their lips the nightly prayer.

' To sleep, however, was out of the question; the whole night through I never
once closed my eyes.

' I rose the next morning a haggard
object enough, and hurried down to the

sitting-room I had occupied the preceding
evening, in the faint hope of finding some
letter lying there which would serve to
relieve my mind of the crushing anxiety
which was bowing me down.

'On entering the room, what was my
surprise to see Mr. Roupe!

'From the expression of his face, I saw
at once that I had no good news to expect.
He rose and, crossing the room to meet me,
took my hand with a look of respectful
regret, as a friend would do who had evil
tidings to communicate.

'"My dear Mrs. Campbell," he said, "it
would be no kindness to keep you longer
in suspense. I have been up to your house
this morning; and I grieve to tell you that
the entire story we were told last night was
an untruth."

'"Then my husband—then my boys?"
I gasped.

'"Pray calm yourself," he said. "I may tell
you at once that there is no distress in your
house—no execution has been put in there.
That subterfuge would seem to have been
invented—I am afraid I must be plain—
invented by Mr. Campbell in order to get
you out of the way while he returned to

the house to complete his preparations for starting."

' " Where—where then is my husband— where are my boys?" I asked in an agony of apprehension.

' " They sailed at five o'clock this morning for Canada," he said.

' What I felt, how I stood this blow, I can hardly now conceive; I dare scarcely recall the dismay and misery of that hour.

' For a long time I sat there helpless and stunned; I seemed not to have a friend in the world.

' Mr. Roupe was very kind. At first he let my sorrow have its way. It was only when he thought, I conclude, from my suddenly ceasing to weep and rising up to go home—home!—that something like indignation against my husband was taking the place of sorrow in my mind—it was only then that he ventured to suggest a remedy.

' Cautiously and by degrees he represented to me the forlorn condition in which I was left, the need I had for some friend who could feel for me as he felt—the tenderest respect and compassion—to fight my battle with the world, to put in force

the full power of the law for the recovery
of my children, and to obtain a divorce
from the husband who had so cruelly
wronged and deserted me.

'I was little used to the ways of the
world, and at first I took all this for the
advice of a friend whose judgment only
was in error. Mr. Roupe did not know, I
thought, that I was too much attached to
my husband ever to think of seeking to be
divorced from him. Something, however,
in his manner struck me as strange, and I
began to suspect that there must be a mistake somewhere. My one desire was now
to hasten home, and judge for myself of
the state of things there.

'Rather abruptly, therefore, I left Mr.
Roupe and the hotel, and hurried home.
A faint hope bore me up, that all I had
been told was a hideous dream, and I should
find Campbell and my boys at home.

'But when I reached my house, no husband and no sons were there. The house
was just as I had left it. No execution
had been put in. The whole story was
indeed a falsehood from beginning to end,
except that part of it which related to the
sailing for Canada. But the falsehood

was not my husband's falsehood, but Mr.
Roupe's.

'I found a letter awaiting me from Neil.

'The contents amounted to this: he had
waited hour after hour in vain for my
return, with such help in the way of funds
as would have cleared him for the moment
of his embarrassments; had at last given up
all hope in the matter; and, pained and
shocked by my desertion of my home, had
carried out his first intention of seeking
with the boys to better his condition in the
New World.

'Now, at last, the truth dawned upon
me. Mr. Roupe could never have met
Campbell at all. The story which had
kept me away from my home while Campbell was vainly waiting for me there must
have been invented for the purpose of
parting us. What other views were enter-
tained by Mr. Roupe I have no means of
knowing—do not wish to know. It was
enough that I had been entrapped into a
seeming desertion of all my duties, and
that husband and children were thus lost
to me for ever.

'You may believe that I was reckless
now, and cared not what became of me. One

thing only I had energy enough to do: that
was to shut my door in that evil man's face,
and then cry—cry hopelessly for death.

'But the man haunted me worse than the
curse of Cain.   I could shut my door, but
I could not bar him from the steps.   He
came again and again.   Not being admitted,
he wrote; but his letters were returned by
me unopened.

'Oh sister! that I could have died—that
I could but have died!   But I was not to
die; I had to live for something yet, I
suppose.   But I lost my faith: I could
not see the purpose of such a life as mine.
All my landmarks seemed suddenly swept
away, and I knew not what holding I had
in the world.

'For a length of time I became a prisoner
in my own house.   I dared not stir abroad,
lest I should meet this fiend in the shape
of man.   I grew sick, wanting the air of
heaven—desperate while I knew he tainted
the air so near me.   So I brought myself
to write to him at last.   What I said I forget; but it did not free me.   He haunted
me and my house still.   Then, as a last re-
source, I fled from it, and hid myself away.

'Sister, you are questioning me with

your eyes. How was it, you would say, that you found me in that man's house? I will tell you.

'I was there, quite innocently, for my children's sake.

'Many, many weary years had passed, when one day there came to me a newspaper having some words written on the margin. I was told in those words that Mr. Roupe was a ruined man. His house was no longer his. His household goods had been seized for debt. His wife—or the woman who passed for his wife—had deserted him; his clerks had absconded. But this was not all. He was under a worse ban still. He had, he implied, compromised himself by some fraud or forgery, and daily expected that his papers would be seized. If I desired, he said, to secure the safety of the deeds which pertained to my sons' annuities, I could go to his house and look them up, without being molested by him, as he had fled into the country, and dared not show himself near any of his old haunts. He said he was truly repentant of the unwarrantable part he had acted towards me, and had no other way of expressing his sense of it than by serving me in this

matter. All he begged further was, that I
would forward to him a letter he expected
was lying at his house for him, and which
would be the signal for his starting off at
once for the Continent, as the last hope he
had of escaping the gallows.

'At first I could not bring myself to
endure the idea of entering that man's
house for any purpose whatever. I dreaded
lest some new pitfall should be prepared
for me. Still, it was important that the
law-papers should be secured if possible.
What, therefore, I at last resolved on, was
to make some inquiry so as to satisfy myself that the case stood exactly as Mr.
Roupe had represented it to me.

'For that purpose I sought an honest old
lawyer of the name of Probin, and employed him to procure me all the information he could in the matter. From him I
learned that Mr. Roupe was really absent;
that his house was watched day and night
by the officers of justice; and that it would
be impossible for him to approach it without being immediately seized upon a charge
of felony.

'Thus assured, I ventured to visit the
house, and to search for the deeds. I had

to go several times before I could find
them, spending some hours each day in the
office.

'There, in that lost man's house, whither
I had gone to secure my sons' papers, you
found me. There, too, my brother saw me,
and was persuaded of my guilt. The
letter you asked me to seek I had no hesitation in taking, as it was yours and not
his, and all his letters and papers would
soon be in hands less scrupulous than mine.
Of course I never saw Mr. Roupe. The
letter he had asked me to forward I had
sent on to him. But I supposed it never
reached him. He had already attempted
flight, was intercepted, and thrown into
Newgate. There he died by his own
hand.'

What a hideous tale of guilt and misery
was this!

But Emmeline was innocent! My Ralph's
sister—the darling playmate of his boyhood, was innocent in thought, word, and
deed.

I laid her poor blighted head upon my
breast; and so we two sat silently, side by
side. I stayed with her as long as I might,
and soothed her all I could. And only

when the time had arrived at which I expected Ralph would be waiting for me,
did I rise and prepare to leave her.

I found my husband awaiting me outside.

He saw that I was trembling, and for-
bore to question me.   But I gave him in a
few words the history of James Roupe's
villany.

' Now, you just heavens,' he cried, ' will
not the grave give me back that man for
one short hour?   I think I am not quite a
monster, but by every living hope I have, I
could tear him limb from limb! '

CHAPTER XI.

A BREEZE OFF THE SEA.

Bless God, my Ella, for the gift he dealeth unto thee,
Amid thy calm and sunny bowers, soft dreams of the
  wild sea :—
And to me, whose glimpses of the land are beautiful as
  brief,
To me, the storm-tossed mariner, the love of the green
  leaf!

O doubly sweet my thoughts of thee upon the surging
  main,
And doubly bright the day shall dawn that brings me back
  again ;
When I snatch the lily blooming—pluck the wild flower
  from the wall—
With my arm around my Ella's neck, the sweetest flower
  of all!   E. L. HERVEY.

WE walked very slowly home. We approached the house in silence, Ralph and I. But no sooner were we in the hall, than he seemed to shake off his anger and I my nervousness.

'Do you feel the air of the house particularly reviving, Grace?' he asked.

'Well, there does seem something very delightful about it,' I answered.

'I am almost superstitious,' he went on. 'I came in from a walk I took down to the village lockup to see a poor devil of a poacher they were going to impound there all day, and when I got back I could not imagine what had come to the house. I seemed lifted off my feet by the rareness of the atmosphere! What do you think was the cause of it, Grace?'

'I do not know, I cannot fancy,' I said. 'But come into the book-room and tell me.'

'Stop, Grace! do not go in there. The book-room is engaged.'

'Engaged!' I cried; 'why, who is there? Is there an angel in the house?'

'You shall judge, when I tell you who is there.'

Ralph led me into the reception-room; and, drawing me to his knee, kissed away the last traces of my trouble.

'Now, my darling little mother,' he said, 'who do you think is come to us? Robert Flemming!'

'God bless him!' I cried; 'then, Ralph,

there *is* an angel in the house!' Has he seen Ella?'

'He has: he is in the book-room with her at this moment.'

'Was he not very much struck with her improved looks? She is very much altered since he saw her.'

'I will tell you all about it. But it is a long story, and I see you are impatient to be off to "his majesty." Wait here a moment, and I will come back to you.'

Ralph did come back in about three seconds. And he did not come by any means alone. He pushed open the half-closed door with a kick of his boot, and presented himself in the opening, with the baby in one hand and a large glass of Burgundy in the other.

'Here, here is refreshment of two kinds for you,' he said; 'you can take either or both, but mind which you swallow!'

For fear of a mistake, I drank the Burgundy off; then I took the baby. Ralph drew his chair beside that on which I sat with the little soul on my knee, and told me the news.

'Flemming got my letter,' he said, 'telling him I thought he had better look after his

ward, for that a handsome young dog of a
nephew of mine was over head and ears in
love with her, and that we lived a little too
near the Border here, in fact could almost
see the geese go home at dusk across Gretna
Green! I found him here, as I tell you,
when I got home from the village after
fastening the poacher *out* of the lockup-
house. Flemming confessed that the news
disturbed him strangely. He felt bound,
he told me, to start off instantly, as he had
a duty to perform by the girl. Oddly
enough, he did not ask to see her. So I
thought I would try the effect of a little
surprise upon them both. I excused my- ·
self to him for a minute; left the room;
found Townsend in the dining-room putting
that Burgundy in the cooler for you, and
sent him off to tell Bell to go in search of
Miss Stuart, and tell her to come to me in
the book-room.'

'Ella rushed into his arms, of course?'

'Nothing of the kind, my love. That
would have spoilt all. No; she opened the
door freely and widely, thinking to find
only me there. But the moment she saw
Flemming she grew dreadfully abashed: the
whole plot seemed revealed to her instinc-

tive woman's wit in a moment. She looked
at me while she half crossed the room to
him; but the moment he approached to
take her hand she fled to me, clung to my
arm, and turned her face to my shoulder.
Flemming looked strangely moved, strangely
bewildered. But he followed her, and took
her hand in his, looking wonderingly at me
for an explanation. A mischievous smile
and nod I gave him as I looked down at the
little fluttered bird on my shoulder seemed
to clear matters up amazingly. He dis-
engaged her gently from her hold on me,
and then I left them.'

'Well, really, Ralph, you surprise me.
I had no idea you had such a talent for
match-making.'

'Positively, I do not think those two
would ever have come to an understand-
ing but for me. Her letters to him would
have opened any man's eyes but Robert
Flemming's. And then, why in the world
did he go on talking in his letters to her
of bringing her rocs' eggs, and walrus's
teeth, and whole reefs of white coral,
and water-sparkles from the falls of
Niagara, and bread-fruit from Otaheite,
and lyre-birds' feathers, and phœnix's tails,

if he did not mean some day to come home
and share some of this food and finery with
her? But, hark! here they come.'

I laid my little sleeper—for he was fast
asleep now again—softly down on my lap,
and gave his nose just a slight pinch to
make it look its best. Hardly had I done
so, when the door opened, and Ella and
Robert came in with that sort of tread
that tells you at once the feet that approach
you are walking on air, with the earth far
below them.

Robert Flemming led Ella by the hand,
just as he used to do. I saw no difference
in the looks with which he regarded her,
from those which used to rest so reverently
upon her young head when she leant upon
him for all the support she had or cared
for in the cold blank world of orphanage
where first he found her. A little prouder
perhaps he looked—a little brighter. The
halo of white light about the Carlo Dolce
face was perhaps a tint warmer from the
reflection cast from those golden locks that
floated towards him, and sunned him with
their glory.

How beautiful they were! What a
freshness and a radiance there was about

them! Yet I thought of poor Walter, and
could scarcely repress a sigh.

'What a group for a painter you three
would make, Mrs. Elphinstone!' said Robert
Flemming, after he had greeted me cordially. 'What dainty little mid is this you
have got here!'

'Oh, look, look!' said Ella, as Robert
took up the babe's hand, 'look, Mrs. Elphinstone, 'he knows his godfather already.'

'Why, if the young dog has not fairly
got hold of your finger, Flemming!' said
my husband.

'Yes; and look, Ralph,' I said, 'the boy
is smiling in his sleep. What a little
oracle he is; he knows the touch of a
friend's hand already. Captain Flemming,
you are just come in time to stand sponsor
to my little Ralph.'

'Really, you do not mean it, though?'
he said. 'Surely it is not necessary. He
looks like a perfect little angel. I should
think he could find his way to heaven quite
well without me. Ella, just look at him!
Dare you touch him, Tit? Are you not
afraid that he will spread his wings and be
off like a young seagull if you spread your
canvas out so close to him? See, you have

stooped over him till your hair tickles his chin!'

Robert Flemming took the offending lock from the babe's face, to which it had strayed. And, as he stood and talked to us of old times, I noticed that it was no longer the girl who twined her hair about his fingers; but the gentle, tender, loving hand of the man that curled the beloved locks round that staff of support he had given her. He set the curls like gold rings upon his fingers; and he took other locks and wove them into bracelets for his wrists. And so busy were his thoughts with those old times when he had saved her out of the wreck of her fortunes at sea, that his arm forgot or did not mind our presence, and closed round Ella's neck; and in the pauses of his happy speech his cheek found the golden head itself, and nestled there, till his own was rayed round with its light; and we knew that in that dawn of love the young saint's head had found at once its glory and its crown.

And now, when we had warmed our hearts all round—fairly sunned them in the light of each others' faces—it was time to begin to think of others.

Ella ran upstairs, and brought down with her Frau Hengler. Frau Hengler's hand and Robert Flemming's hand came together with a clash like cymbals! It made the room quite musical. Ella was determined that their talk should not be interrupted; so, seeing me about to rise, she took the babe from me, and sat herself down with it in her lap on a low stool at Robert's feet.

It was really surprising to note how Robert Flemming admired that baby of mine! He never took his eyes off it till we were called to luncheon. Then he took it out of Ella's arms, kissed it, and made it over to Frau Hengler.

Ralph snatched at my arm to lead me in. Ella took Robert's hand of her own accord. What could Robert do?

'Look at this little creature, Mrs. Elphinstone!' he said, just in his own old way. 'What am I to do with her?'

'Set her at your table-head, Flemming, as I have set this plague of mine,' said my husband, 'and make the best of it!'

As soon as luncheon was over, I prepared to keep my appointment and meet Walter in the Hermitage.

I now, therefore, told Ella to act as pilot to
her sailor-lover, show him all the prettiest
nooks and corners about the Grange, "and
make him as happy as a sea-king. Then
taking my Ralph aside, I told him he must
go with me to within a short distance of the
Hermitage; drop behind while I went forward to put an end to poor Walter's hopes;
and remain within call, so that he could
be summoned by me at the right moment,
and take my place by Walter's side, reason
with him, and reconcile him to the loss
of Ella. To tell him that tale about his
mother was of course impossible for Ralph
to do at such a moment.

All my arrangements, however, were
knocked on the head by the unloverlike
persistence of these two, Robert and Ella,
to stick fast by us. We had not got far
when the two overtook us, and were not to
be shaken off.

We had reached to within a short distance
of the Hermitage, and I was on the point of
excusing myself to the young people on the
plea of an appointment there, when Walter,
who had no doubt been long on the lookout
for me, caught sight of Captain Flemming.

In a moment he had sprung forward and seized his friend's hand.

'Flemming,' he cried, 'for God's sake speak out at once! Have I a hope or have I not?'

'Walter,' answered Robert Flemming, 'I am heartily glad to see you, old shipmate. But you take me a little by surprise.'

'I cannot help it. I cannot bear this suspense. Will you give me your ward? Will you give me Ella? I love her. She is mine—she shall be mine. Tell me what you ask of me, and I will go through fire and water for her!'

Ella had shrunk back before the vehemence of this passionate young lover. She had not dropped her Robert's hand, but hung back to the full extent of his arm, with her face turned away.

Robert Flemming looked back at her, and seemed at a loss how to answer her suitor. But he spoke at last.

'Walter, you distress her,' he said, very calmly. 'How can you do this? Choose some other time, man! Look at her! Nay, rather turn your eyes another way. My poor little girl is troubled.'

As he said this, Robert Flemming drew her softly to his side, that she might nestle her head against him. .

'I cannot part with this little creature, Walter,' he said; 'she is all I have in the world. I found her very forlorn—quite a poor little waif at sea. I put her away with strangers once, and she almost broke her young heart. I brought her back again, and she clung to me, just as you see her cling now. She was my pretty plaything, no more. Look how young and tender she is even now. Look at her bright young head, and pity her. How can you be so rough with her? Walter, you have never parted with her as I have; you cannot tell what it is to have known all her sweetness, and to have missed her. I have. I parted with her a second time; and then I knew all I had lost. When I joined my ship, leaving her behind on dry land—when I looked over the gangway I seemed to see her golden hair sweeping under the tides. It seemed to me that she was drowned—drowned by my hand; and I had lost her in the deep water.'

There was just a moment's pause, as Robert Flemming dropped his face to the girl's, and laid his comforting cheek against hers. There was a moment's struggle between the generous and the selfish sides of Walter's nature; but the generous side won it. His voice faltered; but his heart stood firm.

'Farewell, Flemming! Farewell, Ella! God bless you both!' he cried with a faltering voice.

And, like a shot, Walter was gone!

CHAPTER XII.

GOLD AND A CHEST.

What is here?
Gold! yellow, glittering, precious gold!

    *   *   *   *   *

O thou sweet king-killer and dear divorce
'Twixt natural son and sire!
    Thou visible God,
That solder'st close impossibilities
And mak'st them kiss: that speak'st with every tongue,
To every purpose; O thou touch of hearts!
                       Timon of Athens.

THE morning following his sudden appearance at Fairfield to look after his ward, Captain Flemming again quitted us, urgent calls of duty obliging him to hasten back to town, in order to show himself the next day at the Admiralty.

'Now,' said Ralph to me as soon as he was gone, 'we must hold a new council together. You and I, my dear wife, have fought all our own battles. Our articles of peace are signed for life. We must league together now to fight the battles of others. Our allies—these boys and their mother—are somewhat wanting in the munitions of war. We must supply them from our stores, lend them our artillery, and help them to grapple with the foe.'

'I am quite ready,' I said, 'but how is the battle to be conducted: at what point is the first charge to be made?'

'Listen to me,' he replied. 'All last evening I was closeted with Walter. You told me you missed me, you exacting little mortal: I declare there is no getting free from your apron-string. I tell you Walter and I had a long talk, and had it all out.'

'About his mother?'

'Yes. And more than that.'

'About his father?'

'Yes, poor Neil Campbell!'

'Then these boys know that Clement Favrel is not their father!' I cried, in some surprise.

'Perfectly well. Do you not remember that it struck you as odd at the time, that Heine, in telling his story to us and Lady Letty, never once called Clement Favrel his father?'

'Of course I do; but I supposed that singular manner of speaking arose out of his anger against him.'

'At the time Heine told us that story, he only suspected the fact. But that very same evening his suspicions were confirmed. Lady Letty, you recollect, at once recognised Clement Favrel as a man she had known all her life; one of the Favrels of Westmere!'

'But how did they lose sight of their father, Neil Campbell; and how came this man, Clement Favrel, to personate him?'

'That is too long a history to go into just now. The boys will tell you the whole story themselves. It is enough for our present purpose that they did lose sight of their father out in Canada for years, and when it was pretended that he turned up again, they did not recognise him.'

'How came the boys to take it so quietly? Why did they not raise heaven and earth to track this man's path abroad, so as to bring home the murder to his door if they really supposed him to be their father's slayer?'

'That is just exactly what they have been engaged in doing ever since we have known them! Heine kept sharp watch and ward

over the man here, while Walter returned
to Canada for the purpose of tracking over
every spot of ground likely to reveal the
hidden mystery there. To Walter, Heine
communicated by letter the confirmation of
their suspicions the moment Lady Letty
recognised the impostor as really Clement
Favrel.   Walter only returned to England
when the chase appeared hopeless.'

'How came they to be induced to adopt
the name of Favrel?'

'Why, Clement Favrel, in representing
their father, Neil Campbell, of course represented that Neil Campbell's wife, their
mother, had disgraced their name; and that
it was advisable they should change it on
their return to England, and pass under
another name, that of Favrel.'

'But when Lady Letty recognised this
extraordinary man as really Clement Favrel,
and when the boys must then consequently
have known positively that the name, instead of being an assumed, was a real one,
and the man therefore certainly not Neil
Campbell, but an impostor, why did they
not convict him to his face at once?'

'O my love, leave Clement Favrel alone
for getting out of a scrape. Heine put that

very question to him on the instant. His
answer was just what we might have supposed, knowing the man as we do. "My
dear boys," he said, "you know nothing whatever of the world — nothing
of London life. It has been my fortune
before now to pass under an 'alias.' When
Leonard—poor Leonard—poor fellow—ah!
I never spoke to you about your uncle
Leonard! you did not know you had an
uncle; the fact is, we quarrelled, and I was
rather sore about him, could not bring myself to speak of him;—when Leonard and
I were struggling with poverty, two pro-
mising youths thrown upon the tender
mercies of an unpitying and sophisticated
world, the prey of society, we dropped the
name of Campbell and assumed that of
Favrel." '

'I can hear the man!' I said; 'that is
Clement Favrel to a nicety. But now what
about their mother?'

'O it is all right. I told Walter that
story about Roupe's cruel device. Poor
boy! he covered his face with both hands
for some time. His heart turned to his
mother from that moment. He has seen
her. I took him in secretly by the back

entrance, as I took you, Grace. I never went through such a scene in my life. I cannot rehearse it: I should break down.'

' And what is to be the issue ? '

' Why, this. The sight of his mother, and the knowledge of her still lingering love for their father, Neil Campbell, has stirred up this youth Walter anew to hound the man Favrel to the death till he gives up his guilty secret. Walter is perfectly furious against him. He has written off to Holly-wood to Heine, telling him all, and bidding him come here without delay. Heine is sure to feel just as Walter feels in the matter. Heine will be equally rejoiced to recover his mother. He too will dog this strange man's steps even more determinedly than Walter. Between the two, my only fear is lest they should take the law into their own hands, and there should be bloodshed.'

' You will be able to control them within bounds, Ralph. Have you told Walter now at last this long-kept secret, that their mother is an Elphinstone? '

' Of course I have, Grace. Had I ever seen any real good in betraying it, I should have opened it all up long ago. When I had no one to serve by confessing to the

fact, there was no use in proclaiming to
the world that I had a lost woman for my
sister, the first of all my family that through
centuries had ever brought a stain upon a
proud name. Now it is different. I can serve
her boys best by assuming the authority
which my relationship to them will give me.
I am their uncle, their mother's brother.
They know that truth now, and I hope they
will be guided by me.'

'God bless you, my Ralph! ever good,
feeling, right, wise, and kind!'

'I did not do it—make this confession I
mean—altogether with a good grace, my
love; so your praise is a little in advance of
my merit. I had to struggle against many
of my morbid feelings before I could bring
myself to that step; for my sister's good
name is still under a cloud. We may believe her, but the world will not.'

'The more your merit in overcoming
your morbid feelings, as you call them.'

'The merit is not mine, but yours, Grace.
I told you I should explain before I came
to the end of my story, how much your
conduct towards me has influenced my mind.
Remembering how nobly and tenderly you
had dealt by me; how you crushed down

your own sorrow when I cruelly wronged you, and wore a constant smile to soothe my remorse; when I thought of all this, could I do otherwise than follow your bright example—and forget self for the sake of others ? '

' That is just like you. But now tell me about the battle. How is it to be carried on, and what is likely to come of it? '

' Clement Favrel must be watched more closely than ever. Kitty must be put upon the scent. The " birdcage " window, too, must be put in requisition for the purpose of watching all his movements.'

' Cannot the law touch him? Might he not openly be charged with the murder? '

' Quite hopeless that, my love. The thing took place in the other hemisphere, dates years back; and besides, a motive is wanting. This man was as poor after Campbell's disappearance as he was before.'

' Had Neil no near relatives who could show this man to be *not* Campbell?'

' No, Neil Campbell was the last of his immediate family. Besides, so many years would change his appearance.'

' But Emmeline and Heine and Walter

could all swear that he is *not* Neil Campbell?'

'It is difficult to prove a negative. If
indeed we could bring Campbell himself
forward—if it could be shown that he was
not dead, as of course he is,—many might
be found who could reasonably swear that
they believed Neil to be Neil. But put
this man Favrel in the prisoner's dock, with
the presumption on the very face of the
case that he is just what he represents himself to these boys—that is, Neil Campbell
under an alias—and there are few who
would risk their oath, who would lay themselves open to a charge of perjury, by
swearing outright that he was *not* what he
called himself.'

' What could induce the man to admit to
me,' I said, ' that these youths were not his
sons?'

' Heaven only knows! It shows that there
is some curious complication in the whole
affair, which time alone can unriddle.'

'Hush, Ralph! Here comes Kitty.'

' Plase, yer honours,' said Kitty, ' what
'll I jist do with this bag o' shiners?'

Here Kitty produced from under her
apron a small orange-coloured canvas bag

such as farmers use for collecting specimens of grain, or to hold their market-winnings. She held it up before my husband's eyes, and Ralph took it from her hand. On looking into it, he found it to contain two hundred sovereigns, good coin of the realm, bearing the mint impress of our third George's head.

'Why, Kitty,' he cried, 'where have you been fishing to fish up such spawn as this?'

'No spawn at all, your honour, though the bag's so wet and slushy, but as good-growed fish as ever come to my net, it is. It's out o' the spout it's come, as sure as the sparrows builds there; and more was the wonder of me to come upon all them gold eggs as me hand was busy pullin' out the old straw and feathers as thought to be for stoppin' the wather and sendin' of it all over the ould roof o' the farm buildin' and maybe making of its way down over the beautiful figure-head a-top o' the "birdcage" windy.'

'Do you mean to say that you found this bag of gold pieces on the roof of the Glebe Farm, Kitty?' asked my husband.

'Sure and I did, thin, your honour; and

more I'll find too, yet, I dare be swore, for
the bird that laid them eggs there 'll have
been laying of plenties more, it's my belief,
in odd corners here and there about, for
nobody but a miserly ould stick of a skin-
flint ud go to pack away good gould in
birds' nests when the poor lies without
blankits on the highways and under stacks
and a-top of stable-lofts; and it's me belief
when a man turns miser he turns that same
right out, and all his blood's coined into
gould pieces, and all his tears goes to nug-
gets, and his flesh to copper savins, till
there's nothing of him left but a bag of
gould here and a bag of gould there, and a
nugget in the coal-hole, and a penny piece in
the tay-kittle, and it 'll all turn up some
fine day under the muzzles o' bull-dogs and
ratcatchers' mongrils, and if the right heir
don't come by it, why the wrong heir does,
and somebody's the bether for it, anyhow,
spite of old hunx and the divil.'

'Thank you, Kitty. I shall keep this,
till I find the right owner. And now, you
may go back to the Glebe. Use your eyes,
Kitty. Look for more gold pieces, if you
will; I make you welcome to that pastime
with all my heart. But I want you to keep

your eyes about you for another purpose, too. I wish you would watch that Mr. Clement Favrel pretty closely, Kitty. We are rather curious to know something more of that gentleman than we know at present.'

'Well, now, only think o' that!' cried Kitty. 'Why, it's little else I do but watch him, your honour, when he's here, which it isn't much he is, for after he's been more than common busy a-turnin' up o' the ground, and burrowin' like a rabbit, and creepin' and creepin' under mould like a blind mole, off he is by coach the next minute o' time, as if he'd dug so deep he'd come upon the Ould 'un, and that same had left his furnice a coolin' and was afther his heels.'

'Do you know how he employs his time indoors, Kitty?' I asked.

'It's my belief he's play-actin' all alone by hisself, me lady, for as sure as sure, when I am a-clanin' the "birdcage" room, I sees him a-stoopin' and a-porin' over a great chest in that room as I'm a-spyin' into across yonder in the Glebe House — the room with the ind windy to spare. And all in a twinklin' he'll butt at his head with

his hand, and then fling out the arms of
him up to the salin', and strut about up and
down like a mad turkey-cock, and the lips
of him wide open, and the face of him all
of a work, and nobody by to see him and
cry over his make-believe with flowers and
feathers in their hair; and nobody to take
the money of the man as stands at the barn-
door, and the house empty, and the pit with
nobody to clap their hands and cry "braver!"
when he isn't a-doin' of his best.'

'You do not know, I suppose, all that
chest contains?' questioned Ralph.

'A dale o' rubbish, it's my belief, your
honour. It's mostly close shut up, that
chest is, and it's got a spring in the lock of
it, for it's many a time I've heard it go snap
of a sudden, when he's heard the bull-dogs
bark, and he's flung down the lid of it to
rush out and see what they'd be after more
than common, a-grubbin' in the ground.'

'Are you sure you never found it left
open by mistake, Kitty?' said I.

'Oncet I did, me lady, and I jist dropped
my ould eyes in for a minute; but amost
all I could get to see before Mr. Clem
Favrel bounced right upon me was an ould
sword all over weather-stains just like the

stone for colour that's under the drip of the iron-water well, the sick folks go to drink by the dingle wood.'

'Anything more, Kitty?' asked Ralph.

'A great crown all jools, a false beard and a skull cap like a bald head, a smashed music-thing—a gittar I think they calls it —with a soldier's sash tied to the top and tail of it, to hould it on the shoulthers, and a book of music, a rotten pear, a nutmeg-grater and two nutmegs.'

'That will do for the present, Kitty,' said my husband, and Kitty returned on her steps.

'The plot thickens, Grace,' he said. 'Setting aside the rotten pear, the nutmeg-grater and the two nutmegs, there is really matter here for curious speculation. Kitty's description, though wanting in some important particulars, reminds me very strongly of that scene in the ' Iron Chest ' in which Sir Edward Mortimer visits the chest in which are hidden the evidences of his guilt.'

'It really would look,' I said, 'as if this man had some damaging evidence amongst Neil's property, else why all this secrecy about it? If he wishes these boys to believe that he is Neil Campbell, one would imagine he would else make an open display of everything that had ever belonged to Neil.'

' There is poor Neil's old guitar, you see,' returned Ralph, ' with his music, poor fellow, and the very sword and sash, I have no doubt, in which he played the part of a mediæval troubadour with his back against that walnut-tree, singing the very heart out of the bosom of poor little Jessaline.'

' I wish Heine were here. He is very determined when once he takes anything in hand. Poor Walter, I much fear, is somewhat unfitted by this unfortunate love-affair of his, for throwing all his energies into the cause.'

' You are wrong there, Grace. The blow has been a heavy one to Walter, no doubt. But it will not go so hard with him as it would have done with Heine. This new absorbing interest in his newly-recovered mother, and his pursuit of his father's murderer, will help to work his cure, for he is taking up the Favrel hunt with all his heart and soul. Already the prey is scented, and the eagles are hovering.'

' Ralph, caution those boys not to be too

rapid—not to make a move till the time is ripe.'

'Right: but when the time *is* ripe, I shall myself " cry havoc, and let slip the dogs of war." '

CHAPTER XIII.

WATCH AND WARD.

How now! a rat?
Dead, for a ducat, dead.
Hamlet.

Two days brought Heine upon the scene of action.

Heine was altered more than we could have conceived it possible for anyone to be altered in the short space of a few months. Marian must have made good use of her time. There was scarcely a trace left of that morbid youth who had made up his mind to be a lunatic on short notice. He was stouter in bulk, more awake-looking, brighter-eyed, and more cheery-voiced than when we had last seen him at the Grange. And now that Walter was a little subdued and saddened by the disappointment of losing Ella, the twins seemed more closely assimilated in mind and manner than they

had ever been before. They were a noble
pair;

> Like hounds of good St. Hubert's breed,
> Unmatched for courage, strength, and speed,

ready to hunt down the prey whenever
Ralph, my king of men, should bid the
bugle sound.

It was really glorious to see how Ralph
hounded them on. He entered upon the
pursuit with them as if the prey were a
'stag of ten,' and rode on his gallant way,
giving something of glory to an inglorious
chase.

Heine's coming was of the greatest possible assistance. Heine always plunged at
once into the heart of a subject. Heine it
was who first suggested the probable *motive*
of Favrel's personation of his father, and
of his sudden resolution to quit Canada for
England. The moment we told him the
whole story of old Mr. Campbell, down to
the finding of the bag of gold by Kitty, he
seemed to strike at the heart of the mystery
at once.

'Clement Favrel,' he said, 'must have
learned from my father this story of the
unaccountable non - appearance of old
Campbell's, my grandfather's, money. He

may, too, have learned from another source
of the probability of hoards of wealth
being secreted about the Glebe; for I remember perfectly well having read a paragraph, copied from one of your country
papers into the ‘ Canadian News,’ in which
it was stated that somewhere in the village
of Fairfield there was a dwelling-house
called the Glebe Farm which was supposed
to be haunted, and which no one could be
found hardy enough to tenant. It was
added that some gold pieces had been found
loose about the garden in various places, as
if newly washed up by the rains.

‘ At the time that my father took us to
Canada, Walter and I were very young.
The first thing he did was to place us both
at a school in Montreal. From the day in
which we parted with him there, it is my
belief that we never saw him again.

‘ Letters reached us from time to time.
But if those letters were written by my
father, they must have been written under
some strange excitement, for they were not
like any writing we had ever seen of his.
The last of these letters that we received,
came to tell us of a new arrangement which
had been made for our removal to a farm

on the outskirts of Montreal. A man of the name of Smitherstore, we were told, would come to pay for our schooling, and take us away with him. The farm had been purchased from this man, who had failed to make it answer. He was, however, to remain on the premises, give us the aid of his farming knowledge, and remain with us till my father could come to undertake the management for himself. That, at least, was the account given to us. The scheme was carried out: Smitherstore came to fetch us, and to the farm we went.

'Years passed on. I and my brother grew seriously uneasy. We had both of us from the first disliked that man Smitherstore. He was a down-looking, gloomy, reserved man; and his manner impressed us uncomfortably. We were lonely and companionless, and we became possessed by a thousand strange fears and misgivings. The fear uppermost in our minds, was that our father must have been long ago waylaid and murdered, and that this man knew it, if he had not himself had a hand in his death.

'It was, therefore, a startling sequence to the thoughts over which we had been

brooding for years, when one night, coinci·
dently with our having turned up again
that old newspaper paragraph touching the
gold found on the Glebe Farm, this man,
whom we now know to be Clement Favrel,
suddenly, without a note of warning, presented himself before us as our father Neil
Campbell.

'We were, of course, prepared to find a
change in our father's appearance after an
interval of so many years ; but we were
certainly not prepared for so signal a change
as we found in him.   Our father had been
slight in figure: this man was stout, wiry,
and muscular.   Our father Neil Campbell
had a forehead so fair, that, as children, it
had been our pastime to count the blue
veins that showed through it: this man was
bronzed like a Red Indian.   Our father had
shaved close: this man's face was one bush
of hair.   Gait, manner, everything seemed
changed; the man's height even appeared
greater than our father's.

'Now, all these changes might *possibly*
be accounted for by natural means.   Years
might lend robustness of figure; some
figures look taller as they increase in bulk;
a fierce Canadian sun might account for

change of complexion; fashion or taste, for the enormous display of whiskers. But there was one difference which nothing could account for. Our father Neil Campbell had a weakness in his left eye. This weakness had gradually caused the pupil of that eye to be drawn towards one corner. With this man there was nothing of the kind! The pupils of both eyes were perfectly in their right position.

'The first thing he did on coming amongst us was to take possession of the farm, sell off everything, and announce his intention of an immediate return to England. He should, he said, pass under a new name—that of his " clever friend, Clement Favrel."

'Now, when I was a child, I had often heard my father speak of his friend Clement Favrel, who was, he said, very like him,— so like that he had himself often been accosted as Clement Favrel, much to his confusion and annoyance. " Clement Favrel," my father would say, " is a deuced clever fellow. Clement Favrel, let him get into what scrapes he will, is never at a loss to find some way of floundering out of them. Clement Favrel will fall upon his feet some

day, when Neil Campbell is gone to his
account." We little thought, when that
name should turn up again, how true those
words would prove!

'We left Canada very hurriedly, and in
a state of perfect bewilderment. The suspicion that this man was not in reality our
father deepened upon us during the home-
ward voyage. We had scarcely got out
into deep water, when the captain of the
sloop was taken seriously ill. At the captain's desire, this man took the command
of the vessel and brought her safely into
port. Our father, we were quite certain,
had never been to sea in his life except
once, as a passenger in that voyage out to
Canada. On arriving in England, our
suspicions met with a startling confirmation, leaving us little further room to doubt
that the man was really Clement Favrel
himself.

'The first thing he did was to seek out
Marian Favrel, proclaim himself to be her
uncle Clement who had settled in America,
and whom she had never seen, and bring
her home to the house he had taken for us
in London!

'Now, if the man was our father, Neil

Campbell, here was an imposture for which there seemed to be no conceivable motive. If, on the other hand, he was really Clement Favrel, as we fully believed, this appearance in his own person was a most audacious admission of his fraud upon us!

'Still, my brother and I kept our own counsel. I soon learned to love Marian: and Walter and I were agreed that we should carefully conceal our doubts and misgivings from her, lest she should withdraw herself to the friendless and comfortless home from which she had been rescued; since only under the belief that we were her cousins, would she have remained under our watchful care. We were the more confirmed in this course, since this new turn of affairs which seemed to prove the man to be really Clement Favrel, and therefore *not* our father, seemed also to point to the fact that he *was* in truth Marian's uncle, and therefore her legitimate protector.

'It may be conceived how all our suspicions as to the probable murder of our father were confirmed, when Lady Lætitia recognised this man as really Clement Favrel himself,—Clement Favrel, the forger of his brother's handwriting — a man, ac-

cording to her account, a most consum-
mate actor, and capable of anything!'

So far Heine enlightened us.

Here, then, was the wanting motive.
Neil Campbell had long ago, doubtless,
given up as hopeless any attempts to recover the property so determinedly alien-
ated from him by his eccentric old father,
and so unaccountably secreted. And this
man, this Clement Favrel, so well known
to Neil, and so like Neil,—this ' friend of an
ill fashion'—perhaps his closest and most
trusted friend,—had wormed all his history
out of him, got at the clue as to the place
of deposit of old Campbell's money through
that paragraph touching the Glebe Farm,
quietly put Neil out of the way, and stepped
into his place, with a view to possess himself of Neil's lost inheritance; securing
himself by the murder of his friend against
any after-possibility of the discovered wealth
being reclaimed by the unfortunate Neil.

This, then, was the purpose of the 'bull-
dogs,' as Kitty called them: regular Cuban
dogs they were, staunch and bloodthirsty,
but with a taste too for the immortal dollar
besides. According to Kitty, it would appear
that the mine worked by means of these

singular canine miners had already yielded
up some of its precious metal; which metal
had no doubt found its way to London or
Paris during those sudden trips of Clement
Favrel's every time the said bull-dogs gave
note of warning that they had 'come upon
something more than common.' That metal
was now in process very likely of being
converted into those bubbles which were
every day heard of as bursting and over-
whelming the blowers, as poor children
are overwhelmed when their soap-globe
vanishes, and there is nothing left but a
vapour which spirts into their eyes, darkens
their vision, and leaves behind it a sting
that blinds them with tears.

Meanwhile, what was going on in the
'bird-cage' room? The mother of these
boys, after the first interview with Heine
was over, (quite as affecting as that which
had taken place with Walter,) was set to
watch the doings at the Glebe House. That
room at the extreme corner of the Glebe
House range of building, together with
its windows back and front, had, as Kitty
had said, an end window besides. Anyone
moving about that room was, to the view
of a person in the 'bird-cage' window, like

a person moving about in a glass case. They might walk about every part of the room, except just that inner side where there was no window, and be distinctly seen all the while.

Thus, Emmeline Campbell, having no longer to look out with hungering eyes upon her two recovered sons, now employed her time in noting well the inhabitant of that room,—tracking, in short, his every movement with the view to gain some knowledge of the pursuits and secret practices of her husband's murderer.

It was a sickening, hopeless task, and she seemed to feel it so. While going through her daily vigil, with her cheek pressed as I had seen it pressed to the edge of the wall by the window, she grew distressingly weary over the work. It was so great a strain upon her sight, that whenever we, any of us, came upon her— and we all, at judiciously chosen times, secretly entered the farm to comfort and keep her company—we found her eyes quite red with watching.

About this time, too, poor Emmeline became all at once singularly nervous. We thought at first that the constant watch·

fulness imposed on her by the pursuit in which we were all alike engaged had been too much for her, coming so nearly as it did upon the excitement caused by her renewed happy relations with her beloved children. But, on regarding her more closely, neither Ralph nor I could feel quite satisfied that that was sufficient to account for her growing uneasiness of manner. She would start at the least sound ; sometimes, when the old walls creaked under a higher wind than usual, as they occasionally did, she would hurry to the door as if she desired to escape from some nameless peril; and was so evidently distressed if we noticed her flurried manner, that we were quite at a loss to conjecture what had come to her.

' Grace,' my husband said to me one evening, when we had cautiously let ourselves out under cover of the orchard trees that embowered the back entrance to the Farm,—' Grace, I hardly think it is right to let Emmeline remain at the Farm any longer. It strikes me very forcibly—now do not be alarmed, my love, but it does strike me very forcibly that something is going forward which makes it dangerous for her to remain where she is. She has clearly seen or heard something which has alarmed her for the safety of her life.'

' Oh, Ralph, if you think that, let us go back at once, and bring her away with us. She ought not to be left another moment there.'

' Wait a moment, my love; just draw up with me under the shade of this apple-tree: I want to ask you a question. Did you, or did you not, hear a very odd creaking noise, something like the breaking away of deal boards, at that end of the long 'bird-cage' room that joins the angle of the Glebe House?'

' Certainly I did. I was about to speak of it, when Emmeline asked me if any more gold had been found on the Farm.'

' Exactly! That remark of hers immediately suggested to me the probable cause of the odd noise I had heard. My belief is, that this wretched man, Clement Favrel, not content with burrowing all over the land he rents of me—the produce of which land, by the way, if it be not farm-produce of his own sowing, but buried treasure-trove, would not lie within his rights, but mine as lord of the manor,—this wretched man I say, my love, not content

with digging up His Majesty's effigies on
his own rented land, is, I almost fear, com-
mitting a depredation on my partition wall,
with a view, I conclude, of making further
and interior search for old Campbell's
hoarded wealth.'

'Why, Ralph, if he is doing that, he may
make his way at any moment into Emmeline's retreat!'

'Well, Grace, that is exactly what I am
afraid of; but I was cautious not to startle
you all at once.'

'Oh, Ralph, she may be murdered!'

'Of course she may—that is, if we leave
her where she is. Come, this will not do.
There is nothing for it, but to bring her
away with us this moment.'

With that, we concluded our whispered
conference, and, turning once more towards
the sheltered farm door, made our way
softly back to the 'birdcage' room.

As we entered, we saw Emmeline crouch-
ing down at the far end of the room in a
listening attitude. She appeared to be trembling violently; and as she looked suddenly
round, surprised by the noise of Ralph's
heavy tread, she clutched at the head of a
sofa for support.

'Emmeline, you do hear that noise, then?'
said her brother.

'Yes, brother, yes, I hear it,' was all she
said.

'Come away, then, with us. You shall
not run this risk one moment longer. This
man is a desperate ruffian, and I must take
other means to bring matters to a crisis
with him.'

'What do you mean, brother?' asked
Emmeline.

I mean, that this man, this gold-hunter,
this man-slayer, is no fit neighbour for you.
You will be frightened out of your life, if
nothing worse. The man seems to have
exhausted the outside of his house, and is
now trying what he can find behind the
wainscots. He may break through the
partition wall in one of his fits of gold-
hunger. Come, put on your bonnet, and
home at once to the Grange.'

'No, brother.'

'Grace, my love, why don't you second
me? Emmeline has got it into her silly
head, I suppose, that your separate welcome
is needed.'

'I am sure she is not waiting for that,'
I said. 'She knows pretty well that I

would walk straight into Clement Favrel's presence and draw him to the Grange by the hair of his head, if such an exhibition would prove my love for you or Emmeline!'

'There, Emmeline, will not that satisfy you? Come; what are you waiting for?'

'For courage, brother!'

'Courage!—Courage to do what?'

'Courage to leave this place of happy memories—courage to part again from the home of my heart's first and last love. I know that I must leave it soon—too soon for me. But till I must, I will never quit it. I am not afraid of this man, Clement Favrel. He may break the wall, he may make his way through, he may murder me if he will: it is here that I would gladly die. Here it was that I first saw Neil. It was a true and honourable love he gave me. He might have betrayed my innocence and my trust: many a man who lives a fairer life before the world, in that world's thinking, would have done so. But he loved me worthily, and he loved me well; and I care nothing what else he was, since he was true to me.'

'Well, well, my poor child, I am not

going to play the corsair and drag you
away. I must stay with you, that is
all.'

'But my sister?'

'Oh, Grace? No, of course I cannot let
her walk alone at this time of night to the
Grange. I will run up to the house with her,
and be down again long before that miserable rat can gnaw through the partition.'

'But there is not an aired bed in the
house for you,' said Emmeline.

'An aired bed! Just fancy a man up-
wards of six feet without his boots going
quietly home and leaving his one sister
alone in a house with a burglar, because
there is not an aired bed with a warming-
pan in it ready for him!'

'But what will you do, brother?'

'Bivouac out under the apple-trees, if
it's a fine night, with the key of the back-
door on my finger; or if it is raining cats and
dogs and live Frenchmen, perhaps, as Grace
has made mes omewhat of a "carpet-knight,"
I may indulge myself with a stretch across
this floor with my soles against yonder
creaking wainscot, and my head in the
"birdcage" window.'

'I would rather you would not stay.'

'What confounded nonsense this is, Emmeline!'

'Pray do not mind me; I am quite safe.'

'Oh, very well, then, the only way is to break through the partition at once. When you find that there is nothing to prevent the man from making his way to your part of the house, you will consent, I suppose, to be removed out of harm's way. Grace, just lend me that poker, will you?'

'For heaven's sake, brother, what are you going to do ? He may be——'

Emmeline stopped abruptly.

'He may be what, sister?' said my husband.

'Behind the partition.'

'Who?'

'Clement Favrel.'

'This is really beyond my comprehension, Emmeline! You believe the man to be there, yet you will neither come home in safety with us, nor allow us to keep guard over you here. Grace, come, my love, I shall see you safe, and then return here to watch over this unreasonable sister of mine, in spite of her folly.'

So home we went; and having seen me in safety, Ralph returned to the Glebe Farm.

CHAPTER XIV.

LOVE AND MURDER.

A murderer and a villain?
A slave that is not twentieth part the tithe
Of your precedent lord?
A cut-purse of the empire and the rule,
That from a shelf the precious diadem stole
And put it in his pocket!   *Hamlet.*

WHEN Ralph came home from spending that night at the Glebe Farm for Emmeline's protection, I found that matters had, during the interval that I had lost sight of him, been progressing fast towards a climax. Ralph came in, and threw himself down on the sofa in my dressing-room, rubbing his hands with glee.

'Grace,' he said, ' we shall unearth this fox yet. He is setting a trap for himself, and if we do not catch him in a felonious act, and have him called to account for that, it is our own faults. If once we have him up

before a court of justice, his antecedents
will get pretty well sifted out of him; and
a charge of burglary will very likely end in
a charge of murder. If he gets off scot-
free on the lesser count—which is not likely,
as I intend that we shall catch him in the
act, take him red-handed—if he gets off on
the lesser count, we shall nail him on the
greater.'

'What have you seen, what have you
done, Ralph?' I asked.

'Listen, my love, and you shall hear.
You will remember that when Emmeline
was pleading so piteously to be left at the
Farm endeared to her as she pretended by
so many loving memories, we were all standing rather close to the partition wall. You
may have noticed too that before I made
that arrangement to sleep on the floor of
the "birdcage" room (I indulged myself with
the sofa after all, so don't look so uncomfortable) I drew both you and my sister to
the opposite end of the room, and that then
I spoke rather low. The reason I did this
was because I suspected, as I still believe
to have been the case, that somebody was
within ear-shot.'

'Who?'

' Why Clement Favrel, no doubt.'

' What makes you think so? '

' I will tell you. When I got back to the Glebe after seeing you safe home, my love, I found Emmeline still looking very distressed. I would say very little to her in the " birdcage " room, and what I did say was not true.'

' Not true, Ralph ! '

' Not true, my love! I told her that I considered she was in no danger, and that I had come to bid her good-night.'

' What was that for?'

' Do you not see? I was talking *to* her but *at* that fellow behind the partition. A stratagem is sometimes necessary in war.'

' Well ? '

' Having done that, I drew my sister outside the room, kissed her and dismissed her to her bed, and returned to the room. Before I entered my little bower of sweets — I could not help thinking of you, Grace, for the life of me—I drew off my boots, then I opened the door very softly and stole in, made my way to the sofa, and lay down.

' I had hardly done this, when those creaking and rending sounds we had both

heard were repeated, more loudly and more
boldly now than before. I lay perfectly
still and listened. The operations going on
so close to me, the rending and shaking of
timber, seemed to promise that before long
I should have the pleasure of a personal introduction to my industrious neighbour.
It was almost a pity, I began to think, that
I had brought nothing with me, no pistols,
not even a stick, wherewith to maul him a
little if he should turn out belligerent.
However, there was the poker, and as the
Irishman said, I had my fists in my
hands.

'This went on for some time, an hour
and a half I should fancy, at least. By that
time the hands which had been so busy at
work would seem to have grown rather tired
of their employment. I thought I caught
the sound of something like a long-drawn
yawn, and after that all was still.

'Now, when I speak of the partition wall
as being where I have described it, at that
far end of the room, you must understand
that the partition itself is not the wall of
the room itself. You will have seen that
there is a door on that side of the room, or
rather at that end of it. Beyond that door

is an open space, beyond that space is the partition.

'Having waited another quarter of an hour or so—holding discretion to be the better part of valour—I took down the key of that door which opened upon the blank space, from the ledge at the top of the door where it was always kept. I managed, though it was rather rusty, to open the door with that key. But I was not much wiser for anything that I could see there. You will have noticed of course that we never burn lights at the Glebe. The days have been pretty long since Emmeline came down here, and she has chosen rather of an evening to be content with the rays from that lamp outside which serves to light up the court and shine in through the window, than to betray her presence by showing a light from within the " birdcage." So I was groping in almost total darkness.

'Very soon, however, I felt my way to the partition. That partition I had nearly stumbled through—which would have been a grievous blunder, as I might have come down with a thump which could have been heard echoing through the Glebe House. The fact was the partition was half broken away, and a man not caring whether he was heard or not, might, by throwing his body against it, fling it down or smash his way through. Not so my cautious neighbour. He would have to work a little more noiselessly and methodically. The work would probably cost him another sleepless hour or two before his end was accomplished. On the following night—this very night that is coming — I have not the smallest doubt but he will accomplish his object, and then we have him on the hip!'

'How will you contrive it?'

'In this way. The two boys will be in the Glebe House. If Clement Favrel has ever had the least suspicion that he is watched by them, they will contrive to throw him off his guard by seeming very studiously inclined, and then going—as he will be led to suppose—very quietly to their beds. So much for the arrangement on *that* side of the partition. With regard to *our* side, the " birdcage " room I intend shall be quite at the mercy of the spoiler whenever he shall succeed in making good his entrance. The door next to the partition shall remain unlocked. He shall have free in-

gress. We will all be on the spot—keeping
perfect silence, mind—to receive him with
full honours.'

'Who do you mean by " all?"'

'You, if you like, Emmeline, and your
devoted soldier, Ralph Elphinstone.'

'But, Ralph——'

'Are you afraid?'

'Not I, Ralph, where you are; but I fear
Emmeline will be nervous.'

'My love, I have taken Emmeline's nervousness into full consideration in making
this somewhat odd arrangement for trapping
a burglar. It would be easy enough of
course to get a couple of constables to watch
for this fellow, in place of a little united
family party like ourselves. But the truth
is, I am not a little uncomfortable about this
nervousness of Emmeline's. It is not like
her at all. She has borne a great deal, and
borne it bravely; yet now, without ap-
parent cause, and when she has her
children restored to her, at last she breaks
down.'

'I think I see what it is, Ralph. I fancy
she dreads the horrible details that will
harrow her soul when once this man is
taken, and the whole dreadful story possibly

got out of him, or his open confession made, of the murder of Neil Campbell.'

'It may be that. The fact is I do not know what to make of it at all: and I do not like to indulge in surmises.'

'How did you leave her this morning?'

'Packing up.'

'Packing up?'

'Yes; she was not aware that I saw what she was doing. I ran up to her dressing-room door to speak to her before I left the Farm to come home here this morning, and so took her by surprise. She looked flurried; and when I asked her what she was doing, she stammered, and at last said, with a manner that seemed scarcely open and truth-ful, that she was preparing to leave the Glebe, to come to us.'

'Of course she was coming to us—of course she *is* coming to us.'

'Perhaps—if she is not first going over the border with Clement Favrel.'

'Ralph!'

'It would not be the first time in her life that she has done that sort of thing, Grace.'

'Ralph, for the first time in my life, I am heartily vexed with you!'

'Grace, people must have something to love.'

'What! her husband's murderer!'

'Perhaps the fellow has persuaded her that he is *not* her husband's murderer—that Neil Campbell fell in fair fight, or that he never met him at all; or that he found him dead, perhaps, got at his papers, and was tempted to encumber himself with Neil's two strapping sons for the chance of one day falling in with the beautiful widow, whose portrait he found in Neil's breast-pocket!'

'What an absurd romance you are weaving, Ralph!'

'Oh, she my have him, my love, if she likes him. It is no business of mine, provided always that he can bring good proof of Neil's being dead, without his having had any hand in that matter—only we must have no more runaway, over-the-border marriages. All I want is to bring the two face to face. All will then be as clear as daylight.'

'She cannot have spoken to him ?'

'I am not so sure of that. There was the door with the key on the ledge; there was the partition wall with a crack in it.

You have not, I conclude, read Shakespeare without being quite familiar with that story of Pyramus and Thisbe?'

'Ralph, have you met Moth and Mustard-seed? Is this your own head upon your shoulders, or is it——'

'Thank you, my love; but I am not "translated" yet. I have grave doubts, and I shall have an eye on my sister.'

'And what about Walter and Heine? I hope you have not bitten them, and made them as rabid as yourself.'

'Yes, I have! They are far worse than I am. There will be no holding them if once they find, on watching Clement Favrel to-night, as they *will* watch him, pretty closely, depend upon it, that he is really breaking through that partition to obtain an interview with their mother.'

'Well, I never heard such a thing as that in all my life! I shall never put faith in Heine and Walter again as long as I breathe!'

'Then I suppose you will never put faith in Ralph Elphinstone again? he is every bit as bad as the boys. But come, love, what better solution of the difficulty can you suggest?'

'I will tell you, Ralph; I see it all now!'
I exclaimed, as the story told me at
Brussels by Captain Flemming flashed
through my mind, giving to my first crude
conjecture the force of conviction. 'Neil
Campbell must be living. He must have
found his way back to England. Nay, he
must be hidden at this moment at the
Glebe; and Emmeline must know it, must
have seen him.'

'Why, good heavens, Grace!' cried my
husband, 'that is a more startling romance
than I was weaving myself. What in the
name of woman's wit has led you to such a
wild notion as that?'

'Emmeline's manner; Robert Flemming's story of the singular disappearance
of Vincent's unknown benefactor behind
the walnut tree fronting the Glebe Farm;
our encounter at Brussels with a man
whose face I did not see, but who, both
from the personal description given by
Vincent to Captain Flemming, and from
my own fancied recognition of the man,
must be the exact counterpart of Clement
Favrel. My supposition would account
for the whole.'

'But if Neil Campbell be hidden at the

Glebe Farm, what should hinder him from coming forward openly?'

'That remains to be seen. He is awaiting possibly the fitting moment for his revenge, just as you and the boys are doing.'

'But Emmeline? Why——'

'Ah, poor Emmeline!' How can she meet Neil after——'

'I see, I see!—that blot upon her name. Still she need not make a mystery about it with us. No; depend on it you are wrong. At any rate, do not let us jump at conclusions.'

CHAPTER XV.

HUNTERS AND HUNTED.

I was with Hercules and Cadmus once
When in a wood of Crete they bay'd the bear
With hounds of Sparta : never did I hear
Such gallant chiding !
Midsummer Night's Dream.

Wouldst thou not spit at me and spurn at me,
And hurl the name of husband in my face,
And from my false hand cut the wedding-ring,
And break it with a deep-divorcing vow?
I know thou canst; and therefore, see thou do it.
Comedy of Errors.

THAT day the war-note sounded for the onset, and the battle was to come off.

Ralph, in harbouring the extraordinary notion which had taken possession of his mind, thought it well not to say too much to Emmeline about the scheme that was in progress of being carried out for the surprise of ' old truepenny ' behind the arras— in other words, for the signal defeat and capture of the stealthy thief who, in breaking down the partition wall that separated his own property from his neighbour's could have but one of two motives—unless indeed he combined his desires. He must be engaged in the covert pursuit either of 'woman or gold,' or of both.

Very much resembling the hunted man, in the mode of our operations, were we the hunters. When darkness fell down upon the Glebe, we, Ralph and I, stole with cautious steps towards the embowed orchard entrance to the Farm. The key was turned as noiselessly in a lock well oiled to receive it, as if a sleeping watch-dog lay close within the door. Ralph, with his feet encased in a pair of old list shoes, led the way along the creaking boards; and I followed upon the heels of my leader with a ghost-like tread.

Reaching the 'birdcage' room, Ralph stepped cautiously in, placed his finger on his lip in token of silence, and beckoned to Emmeline to come and speak to him outside in the passage. It was hardly necessary to do this, seeing that the door by which we entered was at the opposite end of that long room from the other door which has been described as abutting on

the partition. We might very well have
spoken just within our door of entrance,
without much likelihood of being over-
heard by anyone concealed beyond the
farther and opposite door. But my husband thought he could not be too cautious.
When Ralph had thus drawn Emmeline
from the room, he questioned her closely as
to whether she had heard the sounds of the
night previous repeated.

'Ye—es,' she said, with some hesitation.
'I have been listening to them for the last
five minutes or so.'

'Now tell me, Emmeline,' said Ralph,
'have you any idea that the man, Clement
Favrel, has observed that this room is
inhabited? Have you been so incautious
as to show yourself at that window?'

'I—I—brother! I do not know; I cannot, indeed I cannot say. Do not question
me. My heart is sick.'

'Then I almost think, Emmeline, we,
Grace and I, had better watch alone. We
have come together, with the full deter-
mination to note that man's proceedings
to-night. He must have worked his way
pretty well through the partition wall,
and——'

'Oh, brother!'

'What is the matter, Emmeline? Do not alarm yourself. The man will come to no harm, I dare say.'

'It is not that, it is not that!'

'Are you afraid of him? Would you rather not face him?'

'No—yes. I will watch with you, brother.'

'Very well; come along, then. But cautiously, cautiously! not a word is to be spoken, remember, when once we are inside that room. You take up your place on the sofa close to the farther door that opens near the partition: if that door should be opened by anyone within the recess, who shall have made their way to it by breaking through that partition, you will in that position be at once sheltered and hidden by the door itself as it swings open. Grace, you will place yourself within the bay of the "birdcage" window. I shall take my stand in the middle of the room, with my back towards this door by which we shall enter. I shall then be in a position to see what our burrowing friend is like, and quite ready either to spring upon and grapple with him the moment he enters; or, should he attempt to escape by passing me and reaching this outer door, to place my back against it, and effectually bar his egress, until I shall have put such questions to him as I shall see fit. On the other side the partition his footsteps will be tracked. Our fierce young war-dogs are on the scent, and will be ready to tear him down should he attempt to beat a retreat by that path.'

'What dogs? What do you mean, brother?'

'Heine and Walter.'

'Heine and Walter!'

'To be sure. If this man be, as we have every reason to believe, their father's murderer, who so fit to hound him to the death?'

'Oh, my God!'

'Come, come, Emmeline; come in with us, since you insist upon sharing our vigil. But, softly, softly!'

We now stole noiselessly towards our several posts of observation.

The work left unfinished· on the previous night, was evidently being now carried on with great vigour. Creak went the panelling, crash went the boards.

Ralph and I looked at one another from time to time, interchanging telegraphic eye-signals. We both looked often and inquiringly at Emmeline, who had sunk down on the sofa in the attitude of one abandoned to terror and despair.

Ralph's suspicions as he looked at her were deepening; I could read that in his face. What my thoughts and feelings were about her, I can hardly say. Certainly they did not point ,in the direction of my husband's suggestion—no, not for a moment.

Meanwhile the enemy's approaches were progressing with startling rapidity. There seemed to be a hurriedness now about the finishing strokes, as if the workman's hand grew eager, and lost its caution in the face of the closely approaching moment of triumph.

A few seconds more, and the last opposing barrier yielded. The wall gave way. A man's foot was heard crossing the limited space between the broken partition and the door. Another instant, and the door handle stirred. The door opened cautiously. A voice quite strange and new in tone to us, and exceedingly sweet and musical, uttered softly the word 'Emmeline!'

Winning no answer, the owner of the voice now stepped forward within the room—seemed instinctively to know where Emmeline awaited him—turned quickly towards her as she started up—sprang forward, and clasped her in his arms!

But the double tramp of Heine and Walter now came resounding through the door this strange visitor had left open behind him: these brothers—these sons, exasperated by the man's audacity, were rapidly coursing on his heels. The wardogs were afoot, fleet, brave, and thirsting for their prey.

Emmeline's ear was the first to catch those sounds.

'Brother — save him — save him!' she gasped; he is—he is innocent.'

It was all the effort she could make, all the words she had breath or sense to utter, as dropping from the clasping arms that held her, she sank back in a fainting fit upon the sofa.

The man's face seemed strange to me in the dusk half-light, so it did to Ralph; its expression was tender as a lover's. But there was no time for thought or question. All Ralph saw, all Ralph heard, was his sister's voice pleading for the man, and appealing to him to protect and save this strange spoiler.

Quick as thought, Ralph seized the intruder by the arm, and without more ceremony hurled him through the far entrance door he had hitherto guarded lest the man should escape through it! There was but just time for Ralph to pass him through the opening, and set himself firmly against the door, when Heine and Walter burst suddenly and furiously in through the partition entrance, and leaped across the room to where Ralph stood guarding the other door, and barring the passage against them.

Now came the struggle. They knew their foe must have escaped that way; and they saw at a glance that their ally had gone over to the enemy, was covering his retreat, and was ready to do battle for his life if need were.

The blood of the gallant boys was up. They made neither pause nor question. Ralph stood between them and their revenge. But have it they would, in spite of him.

Walter seized my husband by the wrist, and tried to wrench him from his position, or wrestle him down. Heine, equally determined and more dogged, caught Ralph's other arm and tugged at it.

They might just as well have beaten their heads against the wall, for any way they made towards thrusting Ralph from his position.

Once, for a brief moment, when Walter leaped like a lithe hound upon Ralph's arm, which had thrown itself like an iron bar across the opening crevice of the door, there was a passing chance that the champion might possibly be beaten in his efforts to maintain his ground. Once too, when Heine kicked at the panels of the door with his foot, the security of the door itself became a question. But Ralph, my king of men! held his own yet.

The struggle lasted but a few moments, yet the battle seemed long to me looking on. Emmeline saw nothing of it. She still lay in a dead calm, where she had fallen on the sofa.

It was positively exciting to me to watch those three—the lion at bay, and the two lithe young leopards leaping and writhing about him. It was Marius against the battle-dogs of Gaul! Yet to an uninterested spectator I have no doubt the whole scene would have appeared wholly unnatural and supremely ridiculous.

But what was it which suddenly put an end to the fight?—what, save the cool and imperturbable face and figure of the contested prey himself, appearing framed within the opposite open doorway at the partition end of the room!

To that door the man had quietly made his way round.

No one besides myself saw the newcomer re-enter, except Ralph.

Quick ever to see his way to the right thing to do at the right moment, Ralph's part was soon taken.

Ralph allowed himself to be ingloriously conquered.

Heine felt him yield, and thought he had overcome him. Walter seeing this, followed up the advantage, and flung Ralph's arm from its position across the door, forced the door open, and dashed through. Heine, without turning to the right or to the left, flung out after him ; both the brothers thus plunging wildly through the door they had battled so stoutly to gain possession of, and disappearing altogether from the scene.

Ralph coolly turned the key upon them.

I was now bending over Emmeline, who showed no signs of coming to herself. I loosened her dress, bathed her temples with some water that stood near, threw open the window, and awaited her return to consciousness.

Meanwhile, Ralph and the intruder for whose safe-keeping he had battled so stoutly, were not silent.

'Will you do me the favour,' said my husband, looking fixedly in the man's face, 'to let me know to whom I am indebted for that very ingenious piece of workman-ship which has resulted in throwing two of my houses into one?'

'My name is Clement Favrel,' answered this male syren.

'Then you are not Neil Campbell?' questioned Ralph.

'Most assuredly not.'

'I shall be still further indebted to you if you will inform me where you left that gentleman last,' said my husband.

'In the depths of a Canadian forest.'

'Alive or dead?'

'Silenced for ever.'

'And your purpose here?' persisted Ralph.

'My right in this lady'—and the man pointed to Emmeline.

'Neil Campbell's death leaves that lady no guardian but me, her brother,' said the Colonel.

'We shall see that. Emmeline!' said the man.

The voice seemed to rouse her at last. She slightly moved her head, turning her half-closed eyes towards me.

'Take me away!' she said, feebly.

'Am I your husband, Emmeline, or am I not?' asked Clement.

'Never—never!' she cried, now fully roused at last. 'Brother—sister, take me home!'

Swift as lightning, my husband's grasp was on the man's collar. It had been only for Emmeline's sake that he had hitherto stayed his hand. For her—at her wish alone—for the man for whom she pleaded and who he was willing to believe innocent if she believed him so, had he battled with her angered sons. But, since then, the

man had, as it seemed, confessed to the
death of Neil; and not only so, but Emmeline now herself threw the wretch off.
Now at last the man was fair game.   And
Ralph seized upon him without a moment's
hesitation.

But Emmeline rose up staggering, and
placed herself between them.

'Brother, brother, loose him!' she exclaimed.   'He has done no wrong.   He
has no fault.   It is I only that am to blame.
I could not tear myself from this spot.
While none recognised him but me, I was
free to feed my heart upon his face.   It is
over now.   You have found your mistake;
and I my sorrow.   Farewell, Neil!'

'Emmeline Campbell,' said this Protean
wonder, 'there are two words go to that
bargain.'

'I will never see you again after this
day—never, Neil, never!' insisted Emmeline.

'Why, pray, my lady wife,' pursued
Clement.

'I am not worthy of you, Neil,' she said.

'Well, that's comical, now?   Who told
you so?   Was it I, Emmeline?'

'All you can say is useless, Neil. I never

will return to you, never share one home with you. There is a stain upon my name. I have been cruelly, most cruelly entrapped, cruelly slandered. By my own acts I gave a colour to the slander. However kindly you may judge me, it is not enough for me that I can give you my simple word that I am innocent. There must be proof of it — clear, unmistakable proof. When I was young and unsuspecting you took no advantage of my ignorance of the world; you gave me an honourable name; you made me your true wife. Neil, my husband, I have never been other than true to you in my least thoughts. But you must not only believe this, you must know it.'

'Suppose I hold the proof?'

'Would to God you did! But it is impossible.'

'Perhaps, my dear, you will allow me to judge of that?'

Emmeline was silent.

Her questioner obtaining no answer, turned to my husband.

'Colonel Elphinstone,' he said, 'if you have no further demands to make upon my coat-collar, perhaps you will allow me to seat myself beside this lady, and try if I have sufficient powers of persuasion left to bring her to reason?'

My husband took my hand, and without making any reply, turned with me to the window.

'Elphinstone, one word with you first,' said the intruder: 'I owe you that. My name *is* what I have told you—Clement Favrel.'

'And Neil Campbell?' questioned Ralph.

'Was an *alias*.'

CHAPTER XVI.

AN UNIVERSAL GENIUS.

He had that kind of fame
Which sometimes plays the deuce with womankind,
A heterogeneous mass of glorious blame,
Half virtues and whole vices being combined;
Faults which attract because they are not tame;
Follies tricked out so brightly that they blind.

BYRON.

RALPH and I seated ourselves beside the 'birdcage' window.

Clement Favrel threw himself down by his wife's side on the sofa by the partition door. So placed, he took possession of Emmeline's waist, and held her prisoner to his will.

Emmeline's head drooped low; her eyes were firmly closed, and her lips rigidly set. But her ears were open; and she could not choose but listen.

'It would be rather a long story, my Emmeline,' he began, 'if I were to begin

VOL. III.   Q

at the beginning. So, I shall skip over
that very agreeable episode in my life when,
having ferreted out my undutiful father,
Perigrine Favrel, who had taken up his
abode at the Glebe under the ill-chosen
alias of O'Neil Campbell — assumed for
the purpose of shaking off his madcap son,
— I found my way beneath a certain "birdcage" window.

' Yonder is the window, graced at this
moment by the fair presence of our esteemed
friend Mrs. Elphinstone, and my hero and
champion, the Colonel.'

Clement Favrel, true to his acting self,
was clearly telling his story as much *at* us,
as *to* his wife.

He went on.

' Let me skip a few years.

' I am afraid, my Emmeline, the less I
say about those years, the better, yet
people should really make allowances for
universal geniuses. I confess to being an
universal genius. What then? The world
could not go on without such aids to its
intellectual development as universal geniuses! They are the very salt of history.
The records your romancist most delights
in, are full of them. People call them

singular.—Singular! Why, they are as common as wortleberries on Westmorland moor, or junipers in Kingley Vale! They are sown broadcast through the land. They were created to flash like meteors across a thousand paths; not to light up a hedge-row here and there, like useless, far-apart, solitary glow-worms!

' So much for your universal geniuses.

' Did you receive the long list of Canadian papers I sent you from the New World, my Emmeline? Yes? Some of them, do you say? Speak up; let me hear your voice; don't be afraid. Yes? Well then, you know, I suppose, how profitably I was employing my time when I left those two pugnacious lads of ours to manage the farm I had purchased out there, under the guidance and direction of its late occupier, old Smitherstore? No? surely you read those flaming notices of the transcendently great singer, Signor Clementi? That was my first venture out there. That was at Quebec—while the boys were at school at Montreal. Next, after they were removed to the farm, I was all the rage in Montreal. There, I assure you, I was considered to be the most refined interpreter of Shake-

speare's comedies ever known. You remember the accounts of those performances
of Favrello's? No? Nor those splendid
literary notices of the new tragedy by "A
Canadian?" Nor the exciting novel by
"Neil-na-Gaellac?" Nor the volume of ex-
quisite poems by "Campbell"? But perhaps
you mistook that name for Thomas Campbell's? Well, he might possibly have written
them—that is, if he had taken pains; but he
did not write them, and I did. Do you
mean to say that you did not read them?

'I begin to think, Emmeline, that you
were almost as inattentive to foreign news
as I was.

'Now, just mark, will you, how little heed
I took of news from England!

'While I was drawing the breath of a
more vigorous life in the New World, bronzing myself under a Canadian sun—for there
is a sun in Canada, though they carry their
winter milk frozen in sacks!—while I was
bronzing myself out of the recollection of
my own sons, and cultivating, with the
same result, it seems, this very handsome
pair of whiskers—I hope you admire them,
Emmeline?—I received a communication
from England. It was certainly the cleverest

piece of lawyer-craft I ever met with. A certain gentleman of the legal profession—don't start!—a certain gentleman of the legal profession wrote me word out there, —though how he came by my address I am at a loss to conceive,—wrote me word that a certain virtuous wife of mine had fallen from her allegiance during my absence. It was a clever hit. But I saw through it. I am not a suspicious man, and not very easily gulled. I consequently failed to do as I was expected to do. I did *not* write to my wife to upbraid her. I did *not* go into heroics, and repudiate her to her face, and throw her on the tender mercies of the man who maligned her, and who trusted to her seeking a refuge in his home when I should finally have discarded her from mine. No, my Emmeline, I trusted that woman; for I knew her.

'But see, now, what puppets we are in the hands of those ill-looking women with the shears—the Fates, you know!

'Just as I was beginning to think of sending for you to come out to me in Canada, and to indulge in visions of my Emmeline's society so long denied to me, a second letter reached me, from the same

quarter as before.   Enclosed was a note in
the unmistakably beautiful handwriting of
that same wife of mine, addressed to that
legal gentleman, and in very plain terms
upbraiding him as the cause of her ruin and
the desolation of her home.

' So there was an end of all my fine castle-
building, as far as the wife was concerned.

' You are growing impatient, Emmeline.
You are trembling, too; I feel you are.
Now, keep yourself quiet if you can, and
listen to me.

' It was at the close of a rather lengthy
engagement out there, that I hit upon a
brilliant idea.   I should tell you, though,
first, that I had been for some years speculating considerably with the funds obtained
by my highly-appreciated theatrical performances ; and, singularly enough, was
anything but successful!   I was, in fact,
much reduced in means ; and so was ne-
cessarily drifted upon the shore of some new
expedient for " raising the wind."   I was
just about to seek out my sons, and take
old Smitherstore's farm into my hands, and
work that vein—for I have an especial
genius for farming operations—when by
the most fortunate accident,--Fortune al-

ways favours the brave, you know!—by the most fortunate accident my eyes lighted one day on a short paragraph in the "Canadian News." It was a paragraph touching this very Glebe Farm—the story of the ghost and all that nonsense, you know. Of course I passed that part of the story over with a smile. Not so, my charming heiress, the account of the gold pieces washed up out of the soil of the Glebe garden. At once I determined to drop my long "alias." There would have been no chance of getting admittance here, you know, as Neil Campbell, the scapegrace son, the lady-abductor, the—the— there, I need not go on with the list of my back-slidings. It is enough to say that I *did* drop the "alias," resume my real name at last, bring my sons over to England, take the Glebe House, and set to work digging.

'But if, at last, I had been obliged to believe that my poor neglected wife—God forgive me!—had found in another the support and protection I had withdrawn from her, there were two generous young fellows, sons of hers, who would *not* believe it. Yet they, too, were convinced at last.

'One day, after a long struggle with himself, Heine went to that legal gentleman's house to ascertain the fact. Poor fellow! he saw his mother coming out of that legal gentleman's house. He hid his face, and he turned back.

'At length matters began to clear up. The legal gentleman had, it seems, turned swindler and forger. Finding his old haunts in London grown too hot for him, down he came here,—little dreaming how close in his new neighbourhood was lurking the man whom he had pursued across the Atlantic with his undesirable pen-and-ink sketches of female character. Here it was that I one day recognised him and pointed him out to Heine. I had long known his pursuits and his haunts perfectly well, though he did not know me even by sight: indeed I was once even fortunate enough, when particularly flush of money, to serve a youth who had been ruined by him. That youth was Vincent Elphinstone. Had I known that our legal friend had been defrauding wholesale his majesty's subjects, and had come skulking down here to be out of harm's way, heaven only knows whether I should not have been tempted—owing him the grudge I did—to turn informer, set the law-hounds on his track, and so help to hunt the wretch down. However, as it turned out, the event served all the ends of justice, both worldly and poetical, without my having soiled my hands in the affair.

' One day, when I had taken one of my usual rapid flights to the great Babel, I was accosted in London streets by an old lawyer of the name of Probin, who enquired if I could favour him with a knowledge of our legal friend's whereabouts. My answer —that he was at that moment down here at Fairfield—was, as the issue proved, his death-warrant. The very next day he was captured, and lodged safely in Newgate.

' In that dark hole—his Newgate cell— the poor devil stumbled at last upon the thing we call conscience. He was there so obliging as to pen me yet another epistle, which owing to my erratic movements never reached me till some months after date; not indeed until I had already discovered that my poor broken-winged dove had found her way back to her own old nest, the " birdcage " window.

' That letter, like the two previous letters,

was penned by no less a person, Emmeline,
than your since defunct friend — James
Roupe.'

A sharp cry—half hope, half fear—escaped from Emmeline's lips.

' Yes, that letter, written but a short
time before the hand which signed it opened
the jugular vein, contained a startling confession.   Emmeline, what are you sobbing
for? Nay, if I am to come back after such a
long absence only to make you spoil your
bright eyes with weeping, I had better go
back to Canada and star it again!

' Come, come, I am not going to distress
you more than I can help.   That letter of
James Roupe's contained the confession of
a scoundrel's device; and—what was of far
more importance—it contained the assur-·
ance of a good wife's loyalty.'

' Neil—Neil! ' cried Emmeline, interrupting her husband, Clement Favrel, whom
still from long habit she addressed as Neil,
—' Oh, Neil—Clement—Campbell—Neil! '
she repeated, falling at her husband's feet,
clasping his knees, and resisting all his
efforts to raise her.

' How many more names, my dear? ' he
said.

'My own—own Neil!' she kept crying.
'Brother—sister, forgive him—love him!
He alone was slow to doubt me. He believed in my truth when all the world was
against me!'

Good heavens! Something was glisten-
ing in Clement Favrel's eyes!

What could it be?

Tears?

That's nonsense!

And yet——?

Every man has a heart—or at least a
piece of one, with a stamp of some sort upon
it. Perhaps it may not be the best current
coin of God's realm, but only a poor, used-
up, battered commodity that will scarce
pass muster from hand to hand. Some men
keep it in their bosoms; too many carry it in
their pockets; with some it finds out a crack
in their brain, into which it slips like a
golden gift into the slit of a child's money-
box, where it is not lost, though it seems
gone for ever. It was into that last place,
that crack in the brain, that Clement Favrel had dropped that heart of his—or what
was left of it. Possibly it will be found
some day; nay, most likely it will be found,
aye, and put to better use than he put it to.

That will be in the day when little children
bring their golden gifts back to the foot-
stool of their Father; and the treasure-
boxes are all opened, and all the world's
wealth is turned out; and the dust and
rubbish that got in through the chinks is
sifted from the pure metal; and all the
sweet and precious things it could have
purchased, but never obtained—for the children did not know how to lay it out—will
be had for the asking; and poor misguided
Clement Favrel will be a child again with
the rest!

CHAPTER XVII.

AN UNEXPECTED ASSAULT.

That is some satire, keen and critical.
Midsummer Night's Dream.

In his brain
* * * * he hath strange places crammed
With observation, the which he vents
In mangled forms.   *As You Like It.*

A plague of opinion! A man may wear it on both sides,
like a leather jerkin.   *Troilus and Cressida.*

'My dear,' began Clement Favrel, when he
had wiped his eyes, 'I am almost inclined
to think I have pretty well sown all my
wild oats. I have really serious thoughts
of sobering down; indulging, in short, in
no more extravagant exploit henceforward
than playing the guitar to you over again,
as I did in the old time, with my back
against yonder walnut tree, and with your
smiling little angel face right before me here
in the "birdcage" window! But you must

keep my father's money-bags cut of my sight, or I shall inevitably relapse! My loyalty to you would, I sadly fear, scarcely be proof against those corrupting miniature portraits of good King George.

'Can a man help his innate tendencies? Is it possible for human nature to control an idiosyncracy? If I have been slightly erratic, pray, my charming Emmeline, whose fault is it? I answer, Nature's! Nature, my dear, was pleased at my birth to bestow upon me a vigorous constitution, a flow of spirits exuberant and perennial; in short, almost too full a complement of animal life. I can assure you that sometimes I have positively not known what to do with it! That ever-developing, boundlessly-growing life of mine actually budded all over me; it made even my language flowery! My days and nights have been one long masquerade ball through it—epergnes on the supper-table, exotics on the staircase, bouquets in bushels, blossoms everywhere—a good many of them bound up in your silken snood, my most extravagantly-adoring, incomparable wife!

'Shall I take my guitar, Emmeline? Would you relish a little serenade under your window? Speak, and it shall be done, my most enchanting, bewitching, soul-delighting piece of womanly perfection!—What the devil's that?'

Here, in the very midst of this wonderful man's raptures, in came Kitty; my husband, hearing a step, having quietly risen and unlocked the door, thinking that the young Favrels were returning.

Kitty, not seeing Clement Favrel, where he had sunk back on the sofa half lost in Emmeline's shadow, came out at once with her errand.

'Plase your honour, the ould coal-cellar's a fallin' in! The wall of it isn't bricks, but it's plasters and laths, and what there is of it's nowhere, for it all come tumblin' down of a lump; and right behind in the place it didn't know how to stick to, agin a brick wall that's not plasters and laths, there's a great big chest fixed in a hole of that same, with a rusty lock and two handles, on a settle, and it's wrote on all in letters as big as the moniment o' Lunnun and as broad as the douwm o' St. Paul's, and the word as I make sense of it, which isn't much it is, is Jess-a-line!'

Up started Clement Favrel as if a bombshell had burst into the room and exploded, and the splinters had riddled him all over.

' Elphinstone, for heaven's sake hold me, will you!' he exclaimed. 'I shall relapse again, as sure as that gold comes to light! I cannot resist it; I swear to you the temptation is too strong for me. At the thought of that chest, that long looked-for treasure, I feel all my old luxuriant animal life come tingling just as it used to do, to the very tips of my fingers!'

Here Kitty made a rush at him.

' If it's houldin' ye want,' she cried, 'it's me that'll hould ye, niver fear, as long as ye like, and maybe longer!' And she threw her great, gaunt, wiry arms about him, hugging him as if she had been a bear.

Clement Favrel's good humour was proof even against this. He only chucked her under the chin.

' My lively little shamrock!' he cried, ' be a little merciful, do now, there's a good soul! See, here is another lady whose arms are waiting to receive me. They are quite strong enough to hold me now, I assure you.'

'Come, Kitty,' said my Ralph, 'we do not want you here just now; you had better march. But just give me the key of that coal-cellar before you go, will you? There, get along with you,' he said, as he gave her a slip of paper on which he had just written some words of explanation in pencil. 'Take that note to Mr. Walter and to Mr. Heine, and tell them to come to us here. Say their mother wants them. You will no doubt find them searching somewhere about the Glebe House for their father. Let Mr. Clement Favrel alone directly.'

Kitty started back, perfectly aghast. She had clearly not had the most remote idea whom she was assailing in that very demonstrative manner. It was enough for her to know that her master's mint in the coal-cellar niche was in danger; and, without a second thought, she had flown at the man, whom she now held as in a vice, about as little dreaming of finding Clement Favrel in the birdcage-room of the Glebe Farm, as of seeing the Pope on his knees in St. Patrick's Purgatory!

Now, however, as her master enlightened

her, she made a vigorous effort to dis-
engage herself.

But though Kitty had done with Clement Favrel, Clement Favrel had not done
with Kitty. He held the strange, gaunt
figure that had rushed upon and tethered
him as with a rope of knotted cords, fast
in his mischievous arms, till he had had his
game out. He took forcible possession of
poor Kitty's lips, and imprinted upon them
a kiss which woke up all the echoes of the
birdcage-room. Then, at last, he let her
go, throwing himself down again on the
sofa beside Emmeline, and laughing till he
cried.

'Och, thin, is it *you* that I've been a-
hugging?' cried the faithful soul, with an
expression on her face of extreme disgust.
'And it's me own lips that'll niver lose the
taste of ye as long as me name's Kathleen
Maguire! Ugh! ye great ugly mountin-
bank! Go to the devil wid ye—in a white
cram'sey waistcoat if ye like!'

Discharging that last shot at her enemy,
Kitty was off; hurtling through the door
as if he had shot at instead of kissed her.

In a short time Heine and Walter appeared.

'My dear boys,' cried their eccentric father, 'let me, before I say another word to you, give you a piece of parental advice, once for all. Whatever you do, never again allow yourselves the indulgence of a fixed idea. There is nothing in all this world so mischievous as a fixed idea. A fixed idea lies at the root of all madness— as far as we would-be wise mortals know anything whatever about that most complicated natural phenomenon. A fixed idea is a luxury I have never permitted myself the indulgence of in all my life. And what has been the result? Why, here am I as hale and sound as the day I was born; and quite capable, moreover, of carrying on the game of life—a little more soberly, perhaps, but quite as healthfully — for the next fifty years or so. Now just see, my dear boys, what a rock you were both of you running your heads against! With that fixed idea of yours, you had all but murdered your own father!'

'You have only yourself to blame, father,' said Walter. 'At any rate do not blame Heine. It was I that was maddest against you.'

'If it had not been for Walter, father,
said Heine, 'I should have struck you
down long before you passed through the
partition.'

'Upon my life,' said Clement Favrel,
'you are two very amiable sons! Hang
me, if I don't like your spirit, boys! I
begin to think there is some of my blood
in your veins, though you are both so like
your mother here.

'I suppose Colonel Elphinstone's note
has opened your eyes? I see how your
mistake arose. No doubt I was a good
deal altered when I came upon you so
suddenly at old Smitherstore's. I suppose,
too, you missed that ugly distortion in my
left eye? No wonder the change startled
you. The fact is, that disfigurement had
caused me a great deal of distress. It
was really no joke to have the "poet's
eye in a fine frenzy rolling" — into one
corner! But I was fortunate enough to
fall in with a marvellously clever fellow in
the medical profession. He showed me at
once that the disorder was curable; oper-
ated upon the eye, and restored the pupil
to its natural position. Strabismus, I
fancy he called it; but we know nothing

about the cure of it yet, he said, on this side the Atlantic.

'So, I hope you believe now that I never was a Scotchman, never was a Campbell, never was a "Sawney" in my life. I hate and loathe the whole cold, cautious, calculating nation of "Sawnies." My father chose to adopt that ill-chosen "alias" of O'Neil Campbell for the purpose of shaking off his hopeful son. I adopted it of course when I found him out at the Glebe. There, under that name, I wooed my pretty Jessaline openly enough as old quidnunc's son; though I took precious good care not to let *paterfamilias* guess what I was about.

'If, boys, you had put the question seriously to me when we were out in Canada, as to whether I was really your father, or only your father's good friend and murderer, I should have made the truth clear to you at once. All this mischief has arisen simply from my first taking an "alias" and continuing to use it as my real name—for King's Bench reasons—and afterwards resuming my real name as an "alias." I was not disposed to let you youngsters into the secret of what I was after in seeking the

Glebe; you wild young colts might possibly not have entered heartily into the
scheme. But when I at last dropped the
convenient name of Campbell in order to
blind others as to my golden motives for
seeking the Glebe; and when I gave you
your real name of Favrel as an " alias," lest
you should let out the secret that Neil
Campbell and Clement Favrel were one
and the same person, I little dreamed
that you would follow out a clue so very
far beyond the end of the thread! True, I
suspected your delusion as to my not being
your father soon after we reached England.
I should then at once have made all clear
to you, but by that time I had a new game
afoot. After that interview with Lady
Lætitia in Colonel Elphinstone's house, when
you sought me, and told me openly that
I was *really* Clement Favrel, which I knew
before, and could not, therefore, possibly
be your father, which I did *not* know
before; when you " denied your father and
refused your name," I saw my way at
once how to take advantage of that queer
little slip. I retaliated, disowned you for
my sons, and led Colonel Elphinstone to
believe that I—a stranger and a Favrel—

was ready, unless bribed to silence, to make public the brand cast, or rather supposed to be cast, by your mother on the Elphinstone name. As Neil Campbell, I could not, of course, have played any such game, since I should not have been likely to proclaim my own dishonour. For the rest, I concluded that you had made the Colonel aware that you were his nephews.

' Allow me here to digress a moment.

' Colonel Elphinstone, upon my word, I must apologise! I beg your pardon heartily, and you really must have won me over in a most extraordinary manner before I could bring myself to say as much. The truth is, I thought you a little Quixotic; and then, being perfectly sure from your likeness to Emmeline, even so early in our acquaintance as that evening when I introduced myself to your notice by sending a little feeler into Lady Letty's scroll, that you were so very near a connection—my own wife's brother, in short—I thought your purse very fair game.

' So much for that.

' Now, my boys! What are you looking so downcast about, children? If your mother can forgive me, I really think you may.

' Are you ashamed of your father?

' Let me read you another moral lesson.
I have learned a good many in my time.
You think, no doubt, you are judges of
character. At this moment you are pre-
suming to judge mine. But, let me tell
you, a man's character—and a woman's
too—is open to many interpretations, as
many as there are minds to interpret it. All
depends on the way you look at it—on the
light you hang it up in. I will give you
an instance, now. There is that softly-
smiling Lady Letty. Your friend, Mrs.
Elphinstone, there, will no doubt tell you
that her ladyship is neither more nor less
than an angel from heaven—an angel in
petticoats, with holes for her wings to go
through! Now, for my part, I think she
resembles nothing more closely than the
sleek, silky marten-cat of our woods, all fur,
and purr, and softness one minute, and all
spitfire and claws the next. That is my
view of Lady Letty. I may be wrong, of
course, and Mrs. Elphinstone may be right;
but one of us two must at any rate be
labouring under a mistake. You see,
then, how a man's actions may be distorted
from their real bent—like a stick in a basin

of water—if you choose to look upon them through the refracted light of your own individual fancy. That is a bad medium, depend upon it.

'You may blame me if you choose for dealing a little hardly with you, my sons, since we three came from Canada. Yet, really, you must confess that you tried me rather severely, for a man of my excitable temperament. Here were you two, both alike determined to make it out that I was not your own father, opposing me in every possible way, and even coolly withdrawing my niece, Marian, from the protection I had given her in downright honest kindness of heart!—perhaps, too, a little out of remorse for an old wrong done to her father, Leonard, my really excellent brother. You must frankly confess that, in this particular case of ours, that detestable cant phrase "There are faults on both sides" holds good. Generally speaking, that phrase is a lie, and one of the most mischievous lies which the world coins to pass off for that rarest of all unalloyed metals—truth. I will give you an instance. When I first married your mother, though there was not a single fault on her part towards me, I was not as kind to her as I should have been. I was disappointed. I supposed I had married an heiress. I found out my mistake; for the gold was not forthcoming. That disappointment I am afraid I vented upon her. Well, now, what would the wise world have said if it could have known what a brute I was? Oh, "faults on both sides," of course! So much for the world's judgments. So much for its cant phrases. If Emmeline opposed me *later*, I had only myself to blame.

'There, I have done. I have tried to throw on you, boys, some of the blame of that fiercely-fought battle amongst us, which has ended in your falling foul of our good friend Elphinstone. Perhaps no one in this life is quite able to say who is wrong and who is right in such battles — in some of their details at any rate. For, *mind*, in what I have been saying I do not for a moment mean to deny one important truth. The greater boundaries between good and evil, my sons, are no doubt strongly enough marked; and may God and your mother, and you, my children, forgive me where I have heedlessly over-stepped them ! '

Clement Favrel paused a moment.

He looked graver, kindlier, gentler than I had ever seen him look.

As my eyes became used to the half-light which pervaded the room, and I was able to discern his face more clearly, I was much struck with its twofold expression. While his head had been raised and its lower features more open to view, his was a face, handsome it is true, but still the face of an ordinary mortal; but when, during that moment's subdued and thoughtful mood, his head was bent down, that face of Clement Favrel's wore an expression such as a painter would give to the highest of the archangels—the broad front instinct with reverence, the lips touched with a divine pity over man's errors and his fall.

'This has been rather a long tirade,' he said at last, shaking off his momentary earnestness, as if he were half ashamed of it. 'I have, however, only one word more to add. Lady Letty thinks I did her a great wrong in my interference with that love affair between her and my brother Leonard. Some wrong I did, I own. I am not going to excuse wholly the part

I acted then. All I can say is, that if it had to be acted again, I should not act so now—that is, if I know myself, which perhaps I do not. Really and truly I did not believe that Leonard cared for anything beyond her money. As for her, she was near thirty. Women do not break their hearts at thirty. I wanted her money, and had no particular objection to herself. She happened to be just then in the furry and purry condition—never showed a tooth or a claw. And, mark you! How was it that I was so blind to my brother's real feelings? How was it that I could so coolly set to work to undermine that pretty superstructure of loves and doves and wedded hopes, which those two were building up so entirely without a thought for my needs of purse and pocket? I will tell you; or rather, I will tell *you*, Emmeline. The fact was, my dear, at that time I had never known what it was to love. No, my Emmeline, I had then never seen your sweet face, my poor, uncomplaining, tender, loving, ill-used, and incomparable wife! '

So!——Let us pray!

Let us pray for Clement Favrel.

One would be disposed here to quote

Scripture, in the parable touching the one against the ninety-nine; but the man's mind, even with so many glimpses of truths as it had caught and clutched at in its perilous drowning course through the world's deep waters, was yet so blinded and so unstable, so tossed to and fro, that one could scarcely say of him yet that he was safe out of the whirlpool.

God help all such ocean strays!

I have known many such. They rarely find their way into lunatic asylums. They generally die comfortably at home in their beds, with weeping eyes about them.

God help them! I say: God help them all!

CHAPTER XVIII.

A MERCIFUL JUDGE.

Alas! alas!
Why, all the souls that were, were forfeit once ;
And he that might the vantage best have took,
Found out the remedy : how would you be,
If he which is the top of judgment should
But judge you as you are ? O think on that,
And mercy then will breathe within your lips,
Like man new made.   *Measure for Measure.*

WE spoke little, Ralph and I, on our way
back to the Grange that evening, for we
carried away with us our two nephews, the
young Favrels, Walter and Heine.
Ralph had proposed that they should
come away with us, for the boys' hearts
were wounded and sore. They were
ashamed of their father and of his antics.
Their affections were wounded, their pride
was hurt. All this might be healed in
time, if this strange man should indeed
cease from his buffoonery, let his unquiet

brain rest, and take only his heart for his guide. Just now it was best that father and sons should meet as little as possible.

'Well, Grace,' said my husband when we were alone, 'this has been a rather startling final scene to our little acted drama!'

'I wish I could think it were final, Ralph,' I said; 'but a man who could convert our sober life-play into such a melodrama as this, may end by making it a tragedy.'

'You think the man is mad?'

'I do.'

'You are much mistaken, Grace. Pray dismiss that terror from your mind. This man Favrel belongs to an extraordinary type of humanity; but he is, as he says himself, by no means a rare specimen. All he wants is poise: when the scales were made, the balance was forgotten; it is simply that, and no more. Common thinkers will see in him only a bad man; but just so, they speak of bad passions. There are no bad passions. There are a good many misdirected ones. So there are a great many men with unguided brains: Favrel is one.'

'But his deception—his vanity—his——'

'Oh, deplorable! There is nothing to
be said for him there. But it is impossible
to account for the vagaries of characters so
complicated as his. Real life abounds with
them; yet fiction would shrink from dealing
with their startling contradictions.'

'Then his heart, Ralph. How could
this man desert first his wife, and then his
children, for a long series of years, after
knowing all her devotion and all their
sweetness?'

'That is difficult for me to answer, my
love. I cannot understand it. But the
thing happens every day. Did you never
see persons of excitable temperament trying to take the legitimate path in crossing a crowded street? Did you never
notice how their quick brains were disturbed
and diverted from the best and safest path
which lay right before them, by the struggle
and traffic, the noise and tumult around
them? I suspect it must be something
like that with such a mind as Favrel's. He
has been quite willing, and no doubt has
always intended, to go straight on in the
orthodox path; but the hum and whirl of
the world about him have been too much
for his somewhat too active brain. He has

become excited, has tripped, stumbled, and got under the horse's heels.'

'How could Emmeline ever become attached to such a man?'

'That man is, I suspect, the only man in the world she could attach herself strongly to. The sympathy btween them is by no means to be unaccounted for. However different they may seem to us, yet they are twin souls, depend upon it. Favrel the spendthrift, Favrel the mad-brained actor, poet, novelist, and rabid speculator, is not the man she married. She married the youth with the guitar, the youth with a real warm beating heart—for I suppose he had one at that time—the youth who, in spite of some few wild oats sown, sowing, and to be sown, came then with his soul on his lips. She kissed it from him, and his soul and her soul became as one. She gave herself not to the man you know, but to his *alias*.'

'It is a pity he has dropped it, then.'

'You are begging the question, my love. He has not entirely dropped it, as you might perceive, if you would look a little closer at him. His other, better self is not utterly discarded. He has found that lost soul of

his precisely where he left it—on the pure
lips of his adoring and devoted wife. If
he appreciates no other virtue in the world,
yet, as you saw, he appreciates hers. He
has, I dare say, lived a not very reputable
life out there in Canada; does not, I will
answer for it, think all women angels; yet
his faith in his wife never wavered for a
moment, till that black villain, Roupe, had
the dastardly wickedness to twist to his
purpose that forlorn letter of hers, written
in a last desperate effort to shake the ruffian
off.'

'I could forgive him anything, I really
believe, but his fiendish game of torturing
Emmeline by threatening to take, and
finally positively taking, her children away
from her, without the slightest cause,
without the slightest provocation on her
part.'

'I think he is wanting—some men are—
in that love for his children, which could
alone enable him to understand what she
must have endured at the thought of losing
them. Let us hope so. Then, you must
remember, too, that there was just that
which to a man like Clement Favrel was
provocation enough.'

' What do you mean, Ralph ?'

' I mean, a secret kept from him — a perilous thing always between husband and wife—as both you and I have known to our cost, twice over; yours about Roupe and mine about Jessaline.'

' But it was a secret kept for the sake of her children. If their father could have found out that a brother of his wife's had given over to her a fortune for her boys——'

' Yes, he would have got at it, and squandered it in some of his wild speculations. Or, if he had found that course rather difficult, as I took good care that he should, he might still have raised money on their expectations, and so ruined them in the end. This is all quite true. The secret was perfectly justifiable. The father not being capable of performing his duty as the guardian of his children, it became the mother's most sacred duty to protect their interests, and so save them from very probable starvation. But that does not alter the fact that the secret being there between them was a sad necessity, and worked mischief, as such secrets always do with those who under other, happier circumstances— the man being an ordinary man and not an

idiot—would have had but one heart and
one soul.'

'You judge this strange man more
favourably than I can do, Ralph.'

' Very likely.   Men are the best judges
of men, women of women.   Take my word
for it, a Protean character .like that of
Clement Favrel's is well worth a patient
study.   I scarcely did him justice myself at
one time.   He has, you see, his impulses of
generosity.   Perhaps you will think it odd,
but I confess that I find many points of
resemblance between your character and
his.   You look surprised.   What I say has
some force, nevertheless.   You may remember that I have before now called you
a " Proteus in petticoats."   It seems to me
that you and this remarkable man have all
along been moving, as it were, in parallel
lines.   Your points of departure, your
moral starting-posts, I grant are wholly
different.   Your paths, too, are widely
apart and could never coalesce; yet their
eventual termination will, it is devoutly to
be hoped, be equally happy.   The scope
of heaven is large enough to include and
embrace them both.'

' I am not sure that I quite follow you.'

'What I mean is this: when you two entered upon life, there were exceptional energies latent in both. The good seed— for I hold all elements of strength to be good—germinated differently, that is all; for good in the good soil, for evil in the evil. To drop all tropes, I would say that that energy of character, that force of will —call it what you like—which with you found its natural outlet in the exercise of all the virtues, with him, found its issue in acts—on which I am not going to sit in judgment. Enough, that in the one case we have a Grace Elphinstone, and in the other a Clement Favrel.'

'Ralph, you are particularly clear-headed to-night.'

'Am I not always a Solon—goose?'

'Men have the better heads after all.'

'I have sometimes suspected as much before now.'

'Oh, it is all very well for me to admit it, just to please a great tyrannical male creature like you; but it is not very gallant of you to insist on it, I must say.'

'You would prefer, possibly, that I should return that little compliment by one in favour of your sex?'

' Yes, to be sure; you might have said a good word for us poor women.'

' Some of you poor women—I am not speaking of you now—are very much what we make of them, I am inclined to think.'

' Ralph, I never heard such a speech as that from you before! Look at your sister. Was it Clement Favrel that saved her from——'

' Yes, it was. He gave her a pure, real, earnest love. He was a god in her eyes, and the temple in which she worshipped him was a sacred one. However he abused her tender trust in him, he yet honoured her above all living women. Being held immaculate by her husband, she never lost her self-respect. As a consequence she never fell into error.'

' Then, too, she was an Elphinstone.'

' Thank you, my love. That is not only another compliment, but, besides, a most Christian example of returning good for evil. It was not very amiable of me to make out you women to be such mere appendages to your lords and masters.'

' I do not care, Ralph.'

' You need not, my love—especially since I hold you to be an exception. Heaven knows, I have myself humiliations enough to confess to! That man Clement Favrel, with all his mad freaks, has exhibited a virtue in which I have shown myself to be miserably deficient. He trusted with a large trust those to whom he was bound.'

'You are good enough for me, Ralph.'

'Grace, I have often told you that you are nearer to heaven than I am. If we two have found a paradise on earth—and I find mine in the air you breathe—yet we are not both native to the place. It was the same in the world's earlier Eden. Adam was only *placed* in the garden, Eve drew her first breath among its immortal flowers! If ever Adam attained to a higher Paradise than that first and fairest garden of the world, it was she, his Eve, who led him thither, drawn by a living chain of them!'

'But the apple?'

'Pooh, pooh! If it stuck in his throat, it served him right!'

CHAPTER XIX.

PARTING AND MEETING.

The clodded earth goes up in sweet-breathed flowers
  In music dies poor human speech;
And into beauty blow these hearts of ours
  When Love is born in each.

Life is transfigured in the soft and tender
  Light of Love, as a volume dun
Of rolling smoke becomes a wreathèd splendour.
  In the declining sun.
                              ALEXANDER SMITH.

WE next had to debate what was to be done with these two youths, Walter and Heine. Heine was all very well with us. But with regard to Walter we were as much puzzled as children are over their game of the fox and the goose and the bag of corn. What with an universal genius—not quite universal enough to win any very idolatrous affection from his sons — at the haunted Glebe, Ella, our little queen of the fairies at the Grange, and Walter standing forlorn between those two mischiefs, we knew not how to ferry the boat over. But Heine came to the rescue.

'I must return to Marian,' he said; 'I am happy nowhere else now. Nothing would have made me quit her for one moment again, but this affair about my father and mother. They seem disposed to make each other happy after their long separation, and we shall only be in the way. We have not the slightest influence over my father, but I think our mother may have some power now to restrain his speculative tendencies. She is no longer suffering under the depressing burthen of her anxieties about us, and I hope she will keep him under a tight hand. Walter shall go to Hollywood with me. I will answer for his welcome with Lady Letty.'

Of course my husband had told them both of the proof of their mother's entire innocence conveyed in James Roupe's confession. That good news had already lightened poor Walter's heart of half its load of trouble; and he was quite willing to accompany his brother to Lady Letty's. One request he made before he went.

Might he,' he asked, 'be allowed to speak
to Ella alone for a few moments ?'

'There, take her, Walter,' said Robert
Flemming, on whose arm she was leaning
when the request was made. 'Go, little
Ella, I can spare you very well, my Fairy
Queen. You do not mind, Ella?'

He bent down and whispered in her ear—

'Be kind to him, Ella. He has loved
you; he loves you still. Comfort him in
all that you can, my little girl. It is a sad
heart-break for him, Ella.'

So Ella shyly allowed Walter to take
her hand and draw her slender arm through
his. And the two went out along the swards
and under the bloomless May-thorns together.

Never so to meet again! Never, while
the world rolls, so to press its sward
with equal foot, and so bask together in its
sunshine; never to look upon the sweet
earth again as now they looked, never to
lift their eyes to the same heaven together!

Such meetings are many under the pitying skies that look down upon us all—
meetings of clasped hands and parted hearts.
Such hours come to many, and God keeps
the note of them, and sets against their

misery the balance of some good, drawn
out of the same scale that holds them. The
misery being too heavy, He takes something
from it, and lays it in our lighter scale of
joys ; till at last, by tender sympathy
with all that in that lighter scale makes up
our due of gladness, the intruding weight
of sorrow, drawn away from its like, becomes even as a joy. A time comes when
the bitterness of such partings passes away,
and the sweetness that lies in the love that
made them bitter once, becomes love's only
part. We can lay the forlorn relic on our
altar of piled-up days .then, a dried, but
sweet-savoured flower. For all other pur-
poses it is done with, save as an offering to
the immortal. It can never burst sheath,
or spread petal again. Its growing is stopped
with the waters that fed it. The heart of
its budding is seared by time, and the bloom
of its beauty is over. But the soul of the
flower remains. It is consumed in the
fire, but the fume of it goes up to the
skies, and life is the sweeter for it, and the
heavens receive it, and God is glorified in
the uprising of that sweet-smelling incense.

It was many a long day before Ella
could tell her Robert how they two, she

and Walter, had fared under those skies so
kindless to her more passionate lover. The
thought of that parting hour was a pain
and a sorrow to her through years of her
young life.

It was long before either spoke.

'Ella,' said Walter at last, 'Ella, have
you forgiven me?'

'I have nothing to forgive, Walter.'

'Yes, Ella. I blamed you—I was very
cruel, very wicked to you. Will you—
can you, forgive me?'

'I was very thoughtless, Walter.'

'You loved—Oh, my God!—you loved
Robert Flemming — then — while I was
heedlessly dreaming that you loved me.
But you were never to blame—never for
one moment, Ella!—I should have seen it
—I should have known it. I have no more
to say—I dare say no more now; it is too
late; it is all over. But I could not go, I
could not leave this place without praying
you to forgive me.'

'Walter, I shall never forgive myself!
But I did not know, indeed—indeed I did
not know.'

'How should you know? I never dared
to tell you till that day I shame to think

of, when I seized your hand so wildly and
held it to my lips. You believe me now?
You believe that I am pained—wrung to
the heart, to think I could so have disturbed and distressed you?'

'Yes, Walter.'

'Would I had never betrayed my heart
to you! A few—a very few hours, and I
should have known all—that you were
Robert's, not mine—his love—his wife!
Oh, Ella!'

'Robert is grieved.'

'Yes I know well he is grieved. He has
a noble—a generous heart. He is worthy
of you, Ella—worthier, far worthier than I
am, of all your love, of all your sweetness.'

'And I—I am very, very sorry, Walter.'

'Your tears are flowing, Ella!—for me—
for me! Oh, my Ella! what a world is this!
Why, why must I part from you!'

'We shall meet again, Walter.'

'Not here—not on this earth, my Ella!
I must lose you; but I cannot see you
another's.'

'You are Robert's friend. You will be
mine too?'

'If ever I can serve you, Ella! Yes. If
ever you—if ever your Robert should need

a friend, call upon me, my sweet Ella. I would come from the farthest end of the earth to serve you—you or the man you love. But I must go now, Ella. I cannot bear to see you near him, leaning upon his arm, looking up into his face. So I had fondly thought you would one day lean on me—so I had fondly dreamed your eyes would one day look up into my eyes— with love, Ella!—with such love as you give to him.'

'He was all I had—he is all I have.'

'Nay, do not try to excuse your love for him, Ella! I know well how tenderly he has cared for you, how unselfishly he has watched over you. If you had not given him a world of sweet affection in return for all his guardian care of you, you would not have been the girl I dared to love. But I was so blind—so blind! I should have known it must come to this. How could he look upon you, and not learn to love you? How could you look into those deep, patient eyes of his, and not see that you were the angel of his life as you were the angel of mine? He will not love you better than I love you, Ella; but you will love him with a love deeper than ever you could have

given to me. I know that well—quite well.
I am passionate and unstable. He is a
rock for you to lean on; and you will lean
on him, Ella, when the waters have flowed
over me.'

There is no prophet like Love!

More than two years later, beneath those
same May-thorns, wandered Ella with a
lover. He was not the same. He loved
her as well as the first had loved her, but
in a somewhat different fashion.

The two had been parted for nearly all
that length of time. Robert Flemming
had joined his ship again soon after his
second flying visit to Fairfield. Now, Robert
Flemming, tired of the 'blue water,' for
the first and only time in his life, was come
back to the Grange.

He had said nothing to us of his having
any particular object in coming to us just
at that time, neither had he to Ella. Perhaps he only longed to wander under the
May-thorns. They were in bloom now.

It was Robert Flemming that walked
with Ella this time over the same path
which had witnessed her parting interview
with Walter Favrel.

Robert's arm was round Ella's neck, and

his head was bowed to her golden hair, just as in the old time. The peace of his spirit was too deep for speech, and his words were few.

'Ella,' he said, at last, 'may I come home?'

She raised her face enquiringly to his, and saw a strange new light bearing down from them upon hers, that she had never seen there before. Luminous was that light and wonderful to her; but they were Robert's eyes; and as she gazed fearlessly into their clear sacred deeps of hallowed light, she saw that the old starlight that had used to shine there, was but a little deepened. The rays that met the quiet light of love in her soul, were not of the stars now, but of the sun.

'Ella, may I come home?'

Now it was strange that, familiar in their affection as these two had been so long, yet, neither at coming or going, at meeting or parting, had the hearts of these two strange lovers met upon their lips. Not even in the days when the child Ella, having lost her Ayah, made Robert do her gentle service, laying her locks in his brown hand to be curled and twisted into golden rings; not even when weary and sleepily resting on his kindly breast, had the child-love in the girl's heart ever offered him one good-night kiss. Robert had never thought of such a thing; why should he? Ella was neither his sister, nor his cousin, nor anything that was his, that he should do so as a matter of use and custom. She was his little foundling, that he scarcely knew what to do with. He would guard her, play with her, watch her with curious eyes as a wonderfully beautiful piece of God's workmanship, cast with the weeds of waters at his feet, to be lifted reverently, and the salt tears wiped away that the rude ocean had drowned it in—that was all: a creature to be reverenced, but not lightly regarded, scarcely fondled, never to be kissed.

' Ella, may I come home ? '

That was the third time of asking. She understood him at last. Either some mysterious telegraph of eye or lip, some gentle closer-gathering fold of the arms she loved to rest in, or else a tender movement towards him in her own young and guileless heart—perhaps both together—told her his intent and wish.

What wish could Robert have that was
not hers too? She had no misgiving, no,
not for a moment, that she could be doing
other than what was right and kind, in
meeting that wish of Robert's, and answer-
ing it fully and freely, the moment she
divined what it was.

Ella turned at once and faced her lover.
Just as she used to do, she lifted her arms
and clasped his neck. But not as she used
to do, did she lean her orphan head upon
his broad shoulder, shut out the wide seas
whose cruel waters had robbed her of all
but him, and find refuge and peace in the
quiet harbour of his breast. No, not so.

Heaven and his face were both before
her. Heaven would not remove, she knew,
but that face had left her for many days,
and might desert her again. She closed
upon it, and secured it with a kiss.

Loving offering on the shrine of love!

Quiet lip met quiet lip. Closer and
closer drew loving heart to loving heart.
No stirring of pulses; no wafting of sighs.
A bird on the May-thorn bough over their
heads, started by no sudden movement, but
rather by the new hush and pause beneath
the loaded branches, darted quickly out

from amongst the embowered leaves, and scattered upon the lovers in its flight a shower of snow-white blossoms. Down on the golden hair and upturned face of the girl fell the virgin shower. Down on the dark locks of the bowed head of the man rained the same crown of stainless white. Nature knew her own; and with the garland of her sweets she drew them each to each, and led them to her bosom like children whom she loved, and would fain clasp both together within her sacred mother-arms, so that neither should be jealous of her fondness for the other.

So a pure heart opened wide its gates, and so a true soul 'came home.'

CHAPTER XX.

HARVEST-HOME.

An angel writing in a book of gold !

* * * * *

'What writest thou?' The vision raised its head,
And with a look made of all sweet accord
Answered—'The names of those who love the Lord!'
'And is mine one?' said Adhem. 'Nay, not so!'
* * * * 'I pray thee, then,
Write me as one that loves his fellow-men.'
The angel wrote and vanished. The next night
It came again with a great wakening light
And showed the names whom love of God had blest,—
And lo! Ben Adhem's name led all the rest !

LEIGH HUNT.

FIVE more years had passed.

My eldest boy, Ralph, was in his sixth
year, and my little Robert close upon his
third, when we held a more than usual feast
at the Grange.

It was the time of harvest-home. There
had been a more than common abundance
of grain that year, a yield that promised
wealth to the rich, and a cheaper and more

plentiful board to the toiling poor. It made my husband's heart glad, and mine too, to see the cheerful faces of the humbler tenants. Their happiness was one of his great desires. Like the rich golden grain full in the fruitful ear, that 'comes of the wayside grasses,' his crown of delight grew out of their humble content.

We always made a feast at harvest-home. The last load carried was the signal for rejoicing. The team, flower-garlanded, rolling smoothly over the stubble straws like a many-flagged argosy bearing its freight of the world's wealth piled from hold to deck, gave musical note of our coming gala. Children blew their horns from the summits of the sheaves—Ralph and Robert amongst the rest, lashed by blue ribbons to Kitty's waist. The village minstrels walked before, at once heralds and musicians. There was, 'Tom, Tom, the piper's son,' himself a piper, and stiff with all his Sunday bravery on. And there was old blind Morrit the fiddler, who had played in the servants' hall at more wedding feasts than there had ever been strings to his fiddle—so often as he broke them by his vigorous handling—since the day, forty years

back, when he bought it a bargain from
pedlar Joe. Many more odd. hands at
harmony besides had come from far to swell
the peal of sounds —an assemblage of dis-
cords by no means disagreeable to us, time,
place, and association considered; but, for
all that, enough, and more than enough,
to have driven a Beethoven mad.

Numerous tables were laid out in the
park. The fare was of the best, and pro-
fuse in quantity. The only difficulty was
to find carvers.

Ralph—he *was* a first-rate carver—took
the head of the centre table; and hungry
eyes above the board, and little kicking legs
beneath it, had not long to wait for the
supplies from that ever open, ready, and
liberal hand. Dr. Percy, too, lent a very
fair hand to the work, at a second table,
assisted by Laurence, Lilian looking on.
You see it always took two to do the work
which Ralph could accomplish with ease,
single-handed! Then, at a third, Mr. Sheringham did his best. His hands were quite
at home; the carvers seemed native to
them. He helped all within his range with
vigorous cut-and-thrust strokes that would
have done him honour at Waterloo. While

that process was going on, he never once
required his handkerchief ball. It was only
when, towards the close of the feast, there
went up a cheer for the gallant hero of
many fights, the lord of that fair manor—
the squire of hearts—that the everlasting
silken cannon ball was set rolling. Then,
indeed, you would have thought that he
held a whole army in either hand, and that
what lay between was the thick of the
battle! Worse and worse, hotter and hotter
grew the fire, when the lady of the feast
was hailed too, with the frequent 'God
bless her!' And when the heir of that
noble carver of feasts (who had made life
such a banquet of joy to me!)—my princely
little Ralph, as like his father as a beam is
to the full sun, came in for his share of the
heart-spoil—(the wee small brother in his
linked hand not forgotten)—then the battle
grew wild indeed! From hand to hand
the missile flew, till there seemed legions
grown out of one; and wondering eyes
from all quarters were turned towards the
silken ball, till it dropped at last from
the battling hands; for the eyes of the
thrower were full, and could see it no
longer.

But what of the other tables?

Vincent Elphinstone took one.

Vincent Elphinstone?

Of course. He and his wife Dora had
returned from India. They had both grown
dreadfully indolent, or they never would
have given Walter Favrel all the trouble
they did in looking after that pretty, merry
little younger sister of Vincent's whom
they had brought to England with them.
She was a very troublesome, awkward
little creature, for ever dropping something; now a rose, now a fan, sometimes,
I fancied, a small tear! What she would
have done without Walter I do not know.
The fan he gave her—rapping her knuckles
with it first by way of gentle reproof for
her carelessness—the rose he shamefully
purloined—the tear——

If a man, a young man, generous and
warm of heart, heart-whole, or with only
a small scar well-healed in the centre of
that heart, should heedlessly make sport
and pastime out of that which is another's
life-earnest; if he should see at last, and
know the havoc he has made in flinging
broadcast in that other's way kind smiles,
tender words, soft grasps of protecting

hands over rough roads and village stile-
ways; laughing sweet defiances in merry
battles for a straw; twinings of white
bindweed flowers among ringleted hair,
gracious sighs over small wound-pricks of
hasty fingers plucking at the blackberry-
fruit; moist eyes over tales of woman's
love—over Mariana's love—or Viola's or
Helen's; meeting fingers over prayer-book
leaves turned together close by an altar,
when the soul is full;—if, we said—Ralph
and I—a young man has thus sown heedlessly, is it not well that he should reap
where he has sown?

In God's name, Walter, dry that tear!

And Walter did. Ruth Elphinstone
never dropped another tear among the
sheaves.

More tables? More carvers?

'Flemming, that table head waits for
you.'

'Elphinstone, here is a little creature
pulling at my anchor-button. What am I
to do?'

'Cut off the anchor-button with the
carving knife, if she will not let go!'

Now, how amazingly like Ralph that
was! The Gordian knot was never a tangle

of any consequence to him—never at least when there was a knife at hand.

Who was that 'little creature?' Not Ella surely? Certainly it was Ella, though; but not the Ella we have hitherto known— though she was there too, of course, a per- fect little mother in miniature. This second 'little creature' of the name had never been to Waterloo. All she knew or cared about that historic name was the glory of it comprised in the wearing of a bright broad ribbon sash, of that colour known to her as 'Wattle-oo-boo.' My little Ralph's hand had taken forcible possession of hers —already, the young rogue!'

What, another table still?

'Favrel, what are you waiting for? Here is a whole fortune in beef and pud- ding, all waiting to be carved into mince- meat. It is quite in your way, I think; you know how to carve, so as to give every- body something except yourself. Fall to the work, man!'

Clement Favrel did fall to the work with zest. He flew at the board as if it had been a Board of Directors! He cut away till all was gone. Then he threw up his head, rolled back, and chuckled!

What had those five years been doing with Clement Favrel? Why, making a man of him. Whenever a new hoard of gold turned up—and hoards of gold were always turning up, some in the drains, some in the waterspouts, more in the garden, more between the coal-cellar walls, a bag or two behind the old granary door, several under the walnut-tree roots, loose coins in old mouse-traps and beer-barrels, a few inside battered hen-coops, one pile heaped up behind the old green slimy water-butt, dozens of small boxes full hidden away under the stair hollows, and others in a long list of out-of-the-way places besides;—whenever a new hoard of this kind 'turned up,' Emmeline served him as people serve children who are having a tooth drawn—she held his hands. So controlled, he bore the wrench tolerably well; and when all was over, and when the gold which he longed to keep but which was best away—like the useful but pain-bringing tooth—was once fairly hidden out of sight and touch, why then she gave him love and kisses as to an unruly child; and he took them, and was thankful. The family treasures, meanwhile, found stored in the great coal-

cellar chest, consisting of enormous piles of
bank-notes, deeds, and bonds, were turned to
good use. Westmere, the beautiful Cum-
berland estate of the Favrels, sold by old
Mr. Peregrine Favrel (Clement's father)
—the entail having been cut off by his pre-
decessor — was, thanks to my husband's
liberal assistance, re-purchased by Clement.
Yes, Westmere was once more the family
seat, and was likely to remain so; for kind
old John Probin insisted upon drawing up
a new deed of entail which secured it to the
young Favrels, Walter and Heine, who, as
twins, would be obliged to inherit conjointly,
as co-heirs. But this is a digression from
the feast: meanwhile the meats are cooling.

Heine, married to Marian five years ago
(Marian was close at his elbow) helped his
father at his father's table. And Walter
helped Captain Flemming at his table.

And Ralph's table? Did no one offer
to take a portion of the labour off his
hands? Oh, he wanted no help; not he!
Poor little Esquimaux-Burlington (his
wife was dead: she died, poor woman, of
gorging herself at a civic dinner, on her
first introduction to the Lady Mayoress)
pottered about him, offering all sorts of

useless fiddle-faddle assistance; and every time he returned to the charge, Ralph sent him off on some small errand or other, out of sheer good nature, to humour his fancy that he was serving his host. Ralph was mischievously twinkling his eyes at me all the time, to tell me that he meant to trot him off yet again and again!

Lady Letty too,—Lady Letty, now on excellent terms with Clement Favrel!—was close by my side; and was much amused to note the telegraphing that was going on between Ralph and me, at the expense of her old enemy, as well as of ' Esquimaux-Burlington.' Ralph's eyes said as plainly as eyes could speak—' Who would have thought when first the man came stalking about our grounds like a sentimental brigand, that the fellow had such a comic vein in him? Did you see how he chuckled over the carving when I twitted him with his besetting sin ?'

Emmeline—or Jessaline, if you like, for we called her as often by one name as the other—was leaning on my arm.

Then, again, there was Kitty. Her eyes, too, were upon us. She came, with her great marching tread, round to where Lady

Letty, Emmeline, and I were standing looking on at the feasting.   Kitty led my two
boys, one by each. hand; and seeing how
my eyes strayed towards Ralph, drew her
own conclusions.

'Ah, me lady!' she whispered, as she
passed on towards another table with my
boys; 'Ah, me lady! it's aisy to see how
it is now betwixt the two of ye.   Oncet it
was with ye just like the swallow-mar-
tins under your eaves, first the one of ye
flyin' off, and thin the other of ye flyin'
off.   All ye wanted was the young birds to
warm the nest.

END OF THE THIRD VOLUME.

LONDON
PRINTED BY SPOTTISWOODE AND CO.
NEW-STREET SQUARE